Success With The Right Queen

Following on from
Success with the wrong queen

Edited by: Oneilia Thompson
Instagram: www.instagram.com/cassiscreative
Personal Instagram: www.instagram.com/kissandrah
Facebook: www.facebook.com/cassiscreative
Facebook Reading Group: Keeping Up With Cass The Author

Check out 'Diary of a savage' By Cassandra Dyer on Amazon kindle.

Please be warned that Cassandra Dyer is a British author, so the spellings of certain words differ.

<u>This book is dedicated to:</u>

My father for his support, wise words and encouragement. Also, for the role he's played in my life; he's always there when I need him.
My mother, for listening to my ideas, excerpts and helping with characters names and for all the support she has given me.

My sister, my neighbour Sophia Toney, friends, family and my readers.

I started writing this book on the 13th of January 2018 and finished it on the 27th of February 2018

<u>This book is part of the 'Love and Success' Series:</u>
Book 1 – <u>Success with the wrong queen.</u>
Book 2 – <u>Success with the right queen.</u>
Book 3 – <u>Success with my wife to be.</u>

Room 101:

Chyna's back slid across the black leather car seat as her body and the Porsche span. Her foot slid off the brake pedal and fell under it, becoming trapped due to her heels. Panicking, but still gripping onto the wheel tightly, she watched her phone float in the air then bounce off the Porsche's window and head straight towards her face. The corner of her phone hit the right side of her top lip and popped it like a balloon. As the Porsche finally came to a halt and crashed head-on into the back of the lorry, the airbag blew up suddenly. The top half of her body flew forward with the seatbelt holding her back. Her face bounced off the airbag as she felt the bridge of her nose crack, followed by a faint crunching sound. The front of the Porsche folded inwards and the brake pedal chopped into her shin shattering it.

***

The Porsche wobbled repeatedly as someone tried their hardest to open Chyna's locked door. Each time the car wobbled, side to side, it woke Chyna up from being unconscious.

"Hello, can you hear me?" A female voice asked before another voice ordered Chyna to,

"Unlock the door!" Unaware of what is happening, Chyna ignored him then slowly raised her head off her left shoulder. She felt her blue curls ruffle against the headrest, then exhaled gently for a few seconds, as her eyes slowly adjusted back to normal. She blinked forcefully double checking that her vision is clear, before she spotted blood on the deflated airbag in front of her. Hearing the car window being thumped, Chyna looked through the window, on her left, to see a woman pointing at the door handle whilst telling her to,

"Unlock the door." She slowly reached for the handle and unlocked the door to hear the same woman say, "We're gonna need you to stay calm. You've been involved in a car accident and help is on the way."

'A car accident?' Chyna said in her head before she felt some warm liquid exit her nostrils. She raised her right hand and tried her best to catch the blood but was unsuccessful. She felt the blood slide down onto her top lip before it dropped onto her navy acid denim jeans. The Porsche door opened and there stood a handsome Somalian man with a well-groomed beard. Before she could panic, he leant inside of the Porsche, reached over her lap and undone her seatbelt.

"Stay calm I'm going to get you out of here." He told her confidently.

"You're not supposed to move them." Shouted a voice from the crowd of tuned in eyes. Ignoring the voice, he squeezed his arm between her back and the chair and tried to scoop her up, until he heard Chyna shriek,

"MY LEG!" before she started bawling, as she felt an unbearable amount of pain travel up her left leg.

"I think her leg's trapped!" The Somalian man shouted to everyone who is watching.

"Someone see where the paramedics are!" The same woman shouted, as she held the door open with a worried expression on her face.

***

With their food trays resting on their laps, Trey and Ayisha are sitting next to each other on the sofa, eating their Chinese and watching 'Naked' by Marlon Wayans.

"I just love the Wayan brothers, they're so creative," Ayisha stated before she bit into one of her egg rolls.

"Yeah, they are." Trey agreed enthusiastically before his phone rang, grabbing his attention. Holding his fork loaded with egg fried rice on, Trey looked over at his phone on the armrest, to see the caller ID is hidden. Not wanting their victory meal to be ruined, he ignored it and continued paying his attention to the television screen. They are both celebrating because Chyna is now officially out of their lives for good.

Without removing her eyes from the screen, Ayisha asked,

"Aren't you going to answer that?"

"Nah," Trey replied then ate some of his egg fried rice. Shortly after his phone rang again. He looked back at it to see the caller ID is still hidden.

"Answer it, it could be someone calling about the gym," Ayisha said optimistically. He nodded as he picked up his phone, unlocked it then held it close to his ear and questioned the person on the end of the line,

"Hello, who's this?"

"Good evening, my name is Isabella and I'm a receptionist at St Thomas' hospital." A voice answered.

Confused and feeling slightly annoyed Trey replied,

"Okay what do you want?"

"Can you please state your first and last name," Isabella asked, needing to confirm who she is speaking to. Trey sucked his teeth then decided to end the call, refusing to cuss her out and let someone ruin his mood.

"Who was that?" Ayisha asked but this time looking directly at him.

"No one." Trey answered then took one of Ayisha's egg rolls from her plate.

"Hey!" Ayisha laughed then watched him take a big bite, eating half. "Was it nice?" Ayisha asked then watched him nod. Before he could eat the rest, Ayisha reached out her arm and slapped it out of his hand playfully. Trey gasped in shock then watched it drop then slide across the wooden floorboards.

"Oh, it's on now!" Trey laughed before his phone rang again. His eyes landed on his screen to see it displayed a professional number this time. "Hello?" Trey answered.

"Hi, this is Isabella from St Thomas' hospital please don't hang up." Feeling frustrated with her, Trey sucked his teeth then removed the phone from his ear with the intent to hang up, until he heard Isabella say, "it's about Chyna Bailey."

He paused then held the phone back by his ear and asked,

"What about her?"

"She was involved in a car accident and needs to go into surgery straight away. We're just calling for your consent to go ahead."

"Oh, okay, of course, go ahead!" Trey insisted.

"Okay, we will get her sent straight into the operating theatre; but because she is under your insurance policy, we have to ask if you're happy to accept the bill?" Isabella asked.

"That's fine I'll pay anything, just make sure she's okay," Trey said as he ended the call and stood up.

Not hearing the whole conversation and jumping to conclusions, Ayisha asked,

"Did something happen to Claire?"

"It's not Claire but I've got to sort something out," Trey said then placed his food down and rushed off. Ayisha removed the tray from her lap then rushed to the door following Trey.

"What happened? Tell me."

"I don't know, but I'll tell you as soon as I find out," Trey told her then rushed out, forgetting to kiss her.

* * *

Fearing the worst, Trey rushed over to the receptionist's desk and introduced himself to the receptionist.

"Hi, my name is Trey Waterhouse, I'm here to see Chyna Bailey."

"Okay, just a sec," Isabella said then took her time to check her computer. He stood there watching her helplessly, hoping she would speed up and stop taking her time. The longer he stood there, the more worried and impatient he became. He battled with himself, wondering if he should tell her to speed up but he decided not to.

"Yes, Chyna's currently in surgery, but there's a note here saying that somebody would like to speak to you," Isabella informed him.

"Who is it that wants to speak to me and why?" Trey questioned her feeling agitated.

"It doesn't say, but if you take a seat, I'll find out for you and let them know that you're here," Isabella told him. She then picked up the hospital phone and began to dial the number on the screen.

"Okay," Trey said then slowly walked over to the waiting area and took a seat with his mind wondering. Shortly after two police officers entered the waiting area and made their way over to Isabella. Sensing a presence approaching the desk, Isabella looked up from her screen, then began to talk to them. Randomly feeling the urge to look away from his phone, Trey looked up to see Isabella pointing directly at him. He wonders why Isabella is pointing at him, then wonders what the police officers wanted as they walk over to him.

"Mr Waterhouse?" One of the officers asked as he held onto his belt.

"Yeah, why?" Trey asked defensively, wondering if this had anything to do with the drugs found at his gym.

"Do you mind if we have a quick chat somewhere more private?" The second officer requested. Hesitantly, he nodded then followed them into a small room, with only a small rectangular window, a table and a few chairs. "Thank you for co-operating with us today, we've just got a few questions regarding the items that were found in your fiancée's car." Once Trey heard this, he immediately felt a massive sense of relief. He exhaled silently and felt his body and shoulders relax.

"Oh yes," Trey nodded then finally took a seat. The first officer sat down opposite Trey, then pressed record on the tape player while the other officer sat straight down and told Trey,

"We found $75,000 cash in a suitcase at the scene of the accident. Do you know of any reason why your fiancée had that amount of cash on her?" Registering the word 'fiancée' in his head sparked an idea. He remembered that everyone still believes they are engaged, so he decided to go with it.

"You know how women are? Chyna had her mind set on paying for her dress in cash, so I gave in and granted her demand."

Not falling for his act one bit, the same officer asked,

"Couldn't she pay by card?" Trey looked at the officers, then spotted the gold wedding band on the officer's finger sitting opposite him. He smiled then replied charismatically,

"Yes, she does but she kept asking to pay by cash, so I gave in. You know, what a woman wants she usually gets."

Still not falling for Trey's charm, the officer reminded him,

"So, what about the other suitcases we found full of clothes?"

Trey stuttered then answered confidently,

"She was going out of town for the dress, and I'm sure from what you've seen, she loves to take care of herself. One outfit is never enough for her. She likes to have options."

"Yes, I can see that," The officer sitting opposite him said believing every word. He then stood up, walked over to Trey and shook his hand while he said, "thank you for answering all of our questions." Trey then stood up and watched the officer move closer to him and heard him whisper, "just a few words of advice, a happy wife is a happy life."

"Advice taken." Trey nodded then listened to the same officer say, "we understand that this is a worrying time for you and that you'd much rather be with your fiancée than here being interrogated. You've answered all the questions we had for you, so go and be with your fiancée." Believing they're done, Trey turned around and headed towards the door, until the same officer asked,

"Don't you want your money back?"

"Oh, yeah." Trey nodded then turned back around to face him.

"It's in holding right now, but we'll get it delivered to your home first thing tomorrow morning. Is the address that we have on the system up to date? Or have you moved?" The same officer asked.

"Yeah, it's the same and thank you, are we done here?" Trey asked desperate to see how Chyna is doing.

"We're good, go and be with your fiancée." The officer nodded then watched Trey leave the room.

Trey re-entered the waiting area and headed straight back over to Isabella. He leant on the desk then said,

"Everything's all sorted now, what's the update with Chyna?"

"Let me just check for you," Isabella said then reached for her mouse and typed in Chyna's full name. As she did this, Trey tapped his fingers on the surface of the desk watching her.

"It looks like she's still in the operating theatre," Isabella told him then looked up from her screen.

"Okay, well do you know how long it might take?"

"I don't know because not all operations are the same. You are more than welcome to wait and once the system has been updated, I'll let you know."

***

Trey's sitting in the waiting area on his phone watching movies and messaging Ayisha. He explained to her that he doesn't know what time he will be back and that once everything is sorted, he'll let her know. A dark shadow stood over Trey blocking the bright white lights shining on him from the ceiling. Seeing this resulted in Trey immediately pausing the film he is watching, then looked up to see who it is. To his surprise, there stood an old Chinese man dressed in a white long coat carrying a clipboard in his hand.

"Hi." Trey greeted him then stood up and pulled his wireless earphones out of his ears.

"Hi Mr Waterhouse, Ms Bailey is out of the operating theatre and is now recovering in her room. She's currently unconscious because we had to work on not only her leg but her face too." The doctor informed Trey.

"Thank you," Trey replied feeling overwhelmed, "can I see her?"

"Yes, of course you can. I will walk with you to her room and answer any questions that you may have." Trey walked next to the doctor, along the white marbled well-lit corridors discussing Chyna's surgery. Wanting to be filled in and to know every single detail, Trey asked,

"What exactly happened and what operation did she undergo?"

The doctor nodded then told Trey,

"Ms Bailey was involved in a serious car accident. She was brought to us with a fractured shin, so we focused on repairing her leg."

"Wow." Trey mouthed as he continued to listen.

"As well as her leg being fractured, Chyna also suffered from a lot of bruising on her face." The doctor paused as they stopped in front of a room that had the number '101' on the door. "This is Chyna's room." The doctor said before he let himself in.

With Trey following, the doctor walked over to Chyna's bed and stood by her side. Standing next to the doctor, Trey gasped at what he saw. There lay Chyna on top of the covers with her eyes shut, in a deep sleep. She is dressed in a loose white bed dress, with navy polka dots on. Her shin is wrapped in a white thick cast that rests on a pile of pillows with her toes poking out. He looked away from her cast to see her blue curls are forced into a loose bobble with her baby hairs dangling freely. He looks away from her hair then spots some scars and bruises on her swollen balloon-like face. He shook his head in disbelief before he noticed a squared fishnet-like white padding that is covering her nose.

"You said just bruising," Trey reminded him then pointed at her nose.

"Yes, I did." The doctor nodded then gently removed the padding from Chyna's nose. Once it was removed, Trey spotted a small red cut running across her curved nasal bone. With his eyes glued to Chyna's broken nose, Trey listened to the doctor explain, "unfortunately, we weren't able to operate on her nose and we won't be able to any time soon. We must wait at least seven days for the swelling to go completely down before we can even think about working on it or referring her."

Not liking what he had just heard, Trey asked,

"But won't she be in pain?" whilst looking directly at him.

"No, she won't be. We currently have her on strong pain killers and will keep her on them until the swelling goes down." Trey nodded then looked back at Chyna and spotted her swollen lips that looked like chunky pink sausages.

"What happened to her mouth?" Trey asked as he pointed at her top lip that has black strings sewn in.

"The impact of her head and the airbag hitting resulted in her lip being split, so we used a few stitches to close the gap. We've got her scheduled in on Friday to get them taken out." Trey sighed heavily as he took everything in. He can't believe the state Chyna is in and knew if she could see herself right now, she would hate it. Seeing her all bruised up and unconscious, made him feel helpless. Trey looked away from Chyna's face to her leg, then walked along the bed to get a closer look.

"What about her leg?" Trey asked as he examined her cast with his eyes.

The doctor took a few steps closer to stand next to Trey then told him,

"We operated on her shin due to the bone splitting. The operation went really well, we predict that it will take up to six months for her leg to completely heal."

"Does that mean she'll be able to walk again?" Trey asked for clarity.

"There are no signs to say that she won't. She just needs to get a lot of rest and keep all pressure off her legs." The doctor paused then told him, "I've got other patients that I've got to see, but if you have any other questions, Chyna's nurse will be around to answer them." Trey nodded helplessly, feeling bad for Chyna and secretly hating himself. He blamed himself for Chyna's accident and wished they resolved their differences differently. Still looking at Trey, and seeing the worry in his face, the doctor placed his hand on Trey's shoulder and told him, "I know this is a worrying time son, but this is only temporary, Chyna will get better soon."

* * *

Trey spent the rest of the day by Chyna's bedside anxiously waiting for her to wake up. While he waited, he spent his time phoning around, hoping to hear an update on his gym.

"Trey?" Chyna called in a weak tone unable to move her lips. Trey removed his eyes from his phone and looked at Chyna, who is looking directly at him. He got up quickly then stood by her side.

"I'm here," Trey told her then reached for her hand and held it. Allowing him to touch her, she looked at him for a few seconds then looked around the room cluelessly.

"Where am I?" Chyna managed to say without her lips moving freely.

"You're in hospital Chyna. You were in an accident earlier today and they had to operate on you." Trey told her calmly, unsure of how she is going to react. Chyna lay there, holding onto his hand whilst staring at him through her puffy half-open eyes. She began to hear the words *'you were in an accident,'* echo around in her head, as she remembered hearing the same thing earlier. Noticing that Trey is looking at her face quite strangely, Chyna pulled her hand away from his then felt her face. She feels her swollen cheeks, then a cloth textured padding resting on her nose. "Trey?" She called in a panic.

"Calm down Chy," Trey told her as he watched helplessly.

"Let me see." Chyna managed to say as she panicked, not liking what she is feeling.

"I think it's best if you don't." Trey advised, refusing to follow her orders.

"Let me see!" Chyna demanded, feeling confused and frustrated.

"But you won't like what you'll see," Trey said, hoping that she'd take the hint.

"Let me see now Trey!" Chyna demanded, losing her patience with him.

"Alright, cool," Trey said. He unlocked his phone that is in his other hand then handed it to her. She clicked on the camera then screamed at her reflection. "I told you!" Trey said then watched her sit up slowly whilst staring at her reflection. She looks at each bruise and red mark, then at her padded nose and stitched lip. She feels her stomach turn, as her reflection made her feel physically sick. Hating what she is seeing and feeling more than embarrassed, resulted in her handing Trey back his phone.

She sighed then said calmly,

"Get out," then hid her swollen and bruised face behind her hands.

"No, I want to stay with you," Trey pleaded, "I want to make sure you're okay."

"Just go!" She demanded as tears ran down her swollen cheeks.

Feeling Trey's presence still in the room angered her even more, so she shouted,

"GET OUT!"

Trey stepped back then told her,

"It's best if someone stays with you."

Chyna sighed behind her hands and begged,

"Please go." He stood there watching her crying, helplessly, wondering if he should leave her or not. With each tear that dropped, pulled at his heartstrings. "Please." She begged then turned away from him and wiped away her tears.

"Okay," Trey agreed then walked over to the door, "get well soon." He said before he took one last look at her then left. He slowly closed the door to room 101, then walked past all the private rooms occupied with patients and their loved ones, which made him remember someone. He stopped in his tracks, then unlocked his phone and searched his phonebook for 'her' number, until he realised that he never had it. Thinking quickly, he decided to have a look on Facebook and search for 'Tyanna'. Once he found her, he messaged her, informing her of everything then asked if she could come to the hospital and be with Chyna, because she needed someone by her side.

***

The sound of a high-pitched ringing sound suddenly went off, as Trey's phone displayed 7:30am. Ayisha stretched then tossed over to face Trey. With his eyes still closed, Trey reached for his phone on the table by his bed, feeling for it with his fingers. Once he felt it, he picked it up and pulled it away from the charger, making it drop onto the floor. Still hearing that annoying high-pitched ringing sound, Trey quickly pressed the 'stop' option.

"Morning," Ayisha said as she stretched again then smiled.

"Morning," Trey said back in his awakening deep voice.

"What do you want for breakfast?" Ayisha asked as usual.

"I'm okay, I'll just have some fruits today. You get your beauty sleep." Trey told her kindly, then moved closer to her and kissed her forehead.

"You sure? I can make you some pancakes." Ayisha offered willingly.

"No, I'm sure, get your rest," Trey told her, then got out of bed and started his daily routine.

***

Ayisha parked her silver Jaguar perfectly inside of an empty space in the gym's car park. She got out, locked it then walked towards the gym's entrance holding onto her handbag and a plastic bag full of freshly cooked warm pancakes.

"Hi lovely, are they in the back?" Ayisha asked the receptionist as she walked over to the desk.

"Hey girl, yes go straight through." The receptionist replied then watched Ayisha walk past her.

Ayisha knocked on the office door then listened for an invitation in.

"Come in," Kaleel called then watched the front door open to see Ayisha standing there.

"Hey Kaleel, how are you?" Ayisha asked whilst walking over to his desk.

"Hey Ayisha, I'm good, how are you?"

"That's good and I'm fine thanks. I'm just here to drop off something for you and Trey to eat." Ayisha told him then sat down and rested the food bag on Kaleel's desk.

"What? Trey's coming in today?" Kaleel asked in a surprised and excited tone.

"Well, yeah," Ayisha replied awkwardly then added, "he should be here already... is he in the toilet?"

Kaleel looked at Ayisha like she is crazy then told her,

"He hasn't been to the gym for about a month now."

Ayisha's jaw dropped to the floor as she gasped, asking hundreds of questions in her head.

"Oh, okay," Ayisha said slowly then stood up before she dismissed herself, "I've got to go."

He watched her pick up the bag and carry it over to the door before he finally asked,

"Can I still have my food?"

"Oh... yeah." Ayisha mouthed then walked back over to him and handed him the bag. "You can have them both."

***

Ayisha looked at the black and white clock that hangs on the wall in the kitchen. It's displaying 5:27pm, which informs her that Trey should be home soon. Ayisha removed the plastic lids from the aluminium food containers, then dished their Indian food onto both plates before she heard Trey's car horn beep twice. Hearing the front door open, Ayisha removed the plate of warm naan breads from the microwave then put one on each plate.

"Hey bae," Trey called cheerfully, then walked into the kitchen to see Ayisha standing in front of the counter, pouring tropical juice into two glasses. He crept up behind her, placed his hands on her hips then kissed her neck.

"Hey," Ayisha replied with an unimpressed facial expression. She then turned around to see a massive smile on Trey's face. Grabbing the opportunity with both hands, Ayisha asked him, "had a good session at the gym?" She watched his smile shrink a bit, then heard him answer,

"Yeah, it was really good."

***

Trey's alarm went off at 7:30am as usual. Ayisha tossed over, waited for him to turn off his alarm, then said,

"Morning, what do you want for breakfast?"

Trey stretched then answered,

"Morning, I fancy a cheese toasty today."

Ayisha nodded then told him,

"I fancy one too," before she got out of the bed.

***

Trey held the front door open and watched Ayisha walk past him whilst telling her,

"Have a good day, with your fine ass," before he pinched it.

"You too, Mr," Ayisha said with a determined look on her face. Trey closed the door behind him, locked it, then got into his car which is parked next to Ayisha's on their drive. His phone connected to his car, via Bluetooth, then began to blast music while he secured himself into his seat with his seatbelt. Ayisha took her time to put on her seatbelt and watched him reverse off the drive from the corner of her eye. Still taking her time, Ayisha slowly reversed off the drive, then waited for his car to turn at the end of the road.

Staying a few cars behind, Ayisha followed Trey, trying her best not to lose him. She has no clue where he is going, or what he has been up to, but after Trey blatantly lied to her face, she knows he's up to something. Still following him, they both head towards Trey's gym, but instead of him stopping and going inside, he drove past like he doesn't own the building.

"Where are you going, Trey?" Ayisha asked rhetorically, then kindly let another car come in front of her.

Still following Trey, Ayisha watched his car indicate, then drive into the hospital's car park.

"A hospital?" Ayisha muttered then followed him. She parked two rows behind his car, then watched him get straight out and walk towards the entrance.Not wanting to lose him, Ayisha quickly got out of the car then followed him into the hospital. She watched him walk straight past the reception desk, which told her that this wasn't his first time coming here. Noticing that Trey is slowing down, Ayisha sat down on the chairs in the corridor, then watched him walk straight into a room without knocking. She felt her heartbeat begin to speed up randomly, without knowing exactly why. Not wanting to confront him out of breath, Ayisha inhaled for four seconds, held her breath for five, exhaled heavily then repeated the same steps. Once her heart beats had slowed down, Ayisha stood up then walked over to the room Trey went into. Ayisha stood in front of room 101, then looked through the open blinds to see a light skinned female with different shades of blue curly hair. Knowing exactly who it is and not thinking clearly, resulted in Ayisha barging into the room shouting,

"WHAT THE FUCK! ARE YOU SERIOUS?" before she marched over to Chyna with her hands out ready to choke her. Sitting on the chair next to Chyna's bedside is Trey, who's looking at Ayisha in complete shock – she's the last person he ever expected to see here. Seeing Ayisha heading towards Chyna with a possessed look on her face, resulted in Tyanna charging towards Ayisha protecting her best friend. Ayisha slid across the floor, to the side, moving out of Tyanna's way which sent her flying past Ayisha. Ayisha then turned around quickly and pushed Tyanna onto the floor. Tyanna crashed onto the floor, landing on her belly, then felt Ayisha grab a chunk of her hair and flipped her over like a pancake, so she is looking up at her. Immediately, Tyanna raised her hands and used them to shield her face, as she raised her leg off the floor and kicked Ayisha in her stomach, which sent Ayisha stumbling back into the wall Tyanna was standing by. Chyna sat there watching in shock, between the gaps in her fingers, as she hid her unrecognizable face behind her hands. She reached for the emergency button then pressed it as quickly as she could, repeatedly. Understanding something needed to be done, Trey finally stopped watching then stood up and rushed over to Ayisha and restrained her. He did this by wrapping his arms around her, gently bear hugging her.

"Calm down," Trey spoke into Ayisha's ear while Tyanna stood up and tried to charge for Ayisha, but the security guards came running and wasted no time in escorting her out of the room.

"GET OFF ME!" Ayisha growled whilst wiggling desperately attempting to escape Trey's grip.

"No, calm down!" Trey begged, refusing to loosen his grip. Her arms are being held by her hips, so she raised her right leg and attempted to kick him in his crotch. "Ayisha stop!" Trey begged fearing for his manhood.

Desperate for Ayisha to calm down, Trey thought quickly then told her,

"Chyna was in a car crash."

"A car crash?" Ayisha repeated then stood still.

"Yeah, look at her," Trey told Ayisha, then watched her slowly look over at Chyna who is still hiding behind her hands.

"Wow." Ayisha sighed then gently wiggled out of his grip. Curious to see more, Ayisha took a few steps over to Chyna's bedside and tried to look past Chyna's hands to examine her face. Not wanting Ayisha to have the satisfaction of seeing her bruised and swollen face, Chyna looked away from her. Seeing a few bruises and the white padding on her nose, Ayisha turned around to ask Trey,

"The crash did that to her face?"

"Yep." Trey nodded then heard Chyna burst into tears. Not wanting to upset Ayisha, but needing to care for Chyna, Trey rushed over to the table, picked up the box full of tissues and handed it over to Chyna. Watching Chyna take the tissues from him, and wipe her face, Ayisha asked in a sympathetic tone,

"So, this is where you've been going?"

Feeling guilty Trey bowed his head and confessed,

"Yes."

"Why didn't you just tell me?" Ayisha questioned him.

Trey looked up then confessed,

"Cause, I thought you'd be mad and not want me to go."

"I probably would have said not to... but seeing her like this... I can see why you've been coming."

"I'm sorry I didn't tell you."

"It's okay... I guess," Ayisha replied then let Trey hug her while she confessed, "I just wish you would have told me."

***

Walking side by side along the corridor, Ayisha decides to ask one of the questions she's dying to ask,

"When did the crash happen?"

Trey cleared his throat then answered,

"The same day we paid her off," then listened to her reply, expecting to be nagged to death,

"The day we paid her off and made her swear to never contact you again... wait... was that why you rushed off during dinner?"

"Yeah, the hospital called me because she's still on my health insurance." Preparing to have his ear nagged off, Trey listened to her say,

"So much for leaving us the hell alone." She laughed then asked, "what happened to the Porsche and money we gave her?"

"Oh." Trey said in complete shock, not expecting for Ayisha to respond so nicely. "The Porsche was a complete write-off and the police interviewed me about the money, I got it back the day after the crash."

"Oh, okay," Ayisha answered, wondering where her money is.

Knowing exactly what Ayisha is thinking, Trey told her,

"Your money is at the house. I was planning on speaking to you about it, but I wasn't sure how to go about it."

Ayisha shrugged then said,

"It's fine. Don't worry about it... I still can't believe how she looks," before she pictured Chyna's face all over again. "She was actually hiding from me," Ayisha laughed. "That's not how I remember her, she seems like a completely different person."

"Yes, she is. She's got no confidence at all."

***

Trey walked over to the till to order their drinking chocolates and chocolate muffins, while Ayisha walked into the seating area to find them a table. Ayisha watched Trey carry over their drinking chocolates and muffins, then place them on the table before sitting down.

"Thanks." Ayisha smiled then pulled one of the drinking chocolates close to her, and held onto it, feeling the cup warm up her fingers. "I still can't get over how different Chyna seemed."

Trey nodded then told her,

"Neither can I. She was worse before the swelling on her nose went down." Trey told her as he reminisced on how self-conscious she is.

"That explains the bandage on her nose." Ayisha said then blew the steam away from her drinking chocolate.

Trey watched her then asked,

"How did you know I was here?"

Ayisha looked up from her drinking chocolate then told him,

"I thought it would be nice to buy you and Kaleel something to eat, so I dropped it off at the gym to find out that Kaleel hasn't seen you in a month." Ayisha told him then looked at him evilly, feeling the same emotions all over again. Trey bowed his head then apologised again, sincerely. "It's okay... I just hope that this is the last time you sneak behind my back. We're partners, I want you to be able to tell me everything." Agreeing with everything Ayisha had just said, Trey reached for her hand, gently pulled it away from her drink then kissed it.

***

As Trey's phone displayed 7:30am, this loud high-pitched ringing sound went off, waking Trey and Ayisha up. Ayisha's heavy eyelids slowly opened, as Trey reached for his phone and turned off his alarm. He placed his phone back onto the dresser, then watched Ayisha move closer to him and rest her head on his chest.

"Morning babe," Ayisha said then heard him yawn loudly.

"Morning beautiful," Trey said once he finished yawning. "What do you want for breakfast?"

"Nuh uh, this time I'll make you breakfast."

"Really?" Ayisha smirked then asked, "what's gotten into you?"

"Can't I treat my lady?" Trey asked.

"Of course, you can! Do I get breakfast tomorrow as well?" Ayisha asked playfully then sat up.

"Aye, don't push it!" Trey laughed then did the same.

"Thought I'd ask." Ayisha laughed then got out of bed and held the corner of their bed covers. Doing the same, Trey got out of bed and held the other corner, ready to help her make the bed. Stepping closer to the bed, Ayisha's feet stepped under the bed and hit something hard. "Ahh!" Ayisha cursed in pain, then sat down on the carpet next to the bed and comforted her aching toe.

"Are you okay?" Trey asked as he watched nervously.

"Yeah, I'm okay," Ayisha said then told him, "I just hit my foot on something," before she reached under the bed to feel for it. Ayisha tapped under the bed, then pulled out an A3 sized photo frame. Refusing to believe what her eyes are seeing, Ayisha helped herself up to her feet, then asked Trey in an annoyed tone, "really?"

Trey stuttered then told her,

"I didn't get around to throwing them out."

"Them?" Ayisha repeated, then dropped the frame onto the bed, knelt back down and pulled 7 more photo frames from under the bed. "You really kept photos of your ex under the bed that we sleep in?" Ayisha clarified in disgust, then threw them onto the bed as Trey watched nervously. He stood there watching Ayisha with the guiltiest look on his face ever. He stuttered on his words, as his hands began to sweat.

"I forgot I put them there." Trey managed to say.

"But why did you?" Ayisha asked in disgust, "why didn't you just throw them out?"

"Because I planned on eventually giving them back to Chyna... Those were taken from her first photo shoot. They're her favourite pictures."

Ayisha sucked her teeth, agitatedly, as she registered what Trey had just said in her head.

"There you go again! You're always being too nice to her."

"I'm not! I get what you're saying, but even you know that she could really do with seeing these right now. Instead of me throwing them out, I could bring them to her and hopefully it will do her some good." Trey suggested.

Wanting to cuss him out, but fighting the urge to, Ayisha sighed then said,

"Fine. I don't want to argue with you, especially not over her!" she paused, then pushed the frames across the bed closer to him, "do what you have to do, Trey." He looked down at the frames, then looked up at Ayisha confused.

"You're not mad at me, are you?" He asked.

"No, I'm not mad. You're a good man with a big heart which annoys me at times. But you've always been like this ever since we were kids... I know you want to help her because that's in your nature, and I know your heart's in the right place," Ayisha told Trey and herself at the same time, "bring them to her, it just might help."

"Okay, I will." Trey replied, then gathered each frame and piled them on top of each other before he asked her, "what do you want for breakfast?"

Ayisha looked at the pile of frames in his hand, then answered in an upset tone,

"Nothing. I'm not hungry anymore."

***

"Knock, knock," Trey said at the same time as he tapped on the door. Not waiting for an answer, Trey opened the door to see Tyanna sitting by Chyna's bedside on her phone.

"Hi!" Chyna called before her cheeks lit up turning bright red. She looks forward to seeing Trey and enjoys his company.

With one hand behind his back, Trey walked over to Chyna's bedside then told her,

"I've got something for you."

"What is it?" Chyna asked the question Tyanna had asked in her head.

"Open it," Trey encouraged her, then pulled a rectangular present from behind his back. Chyna took the present from him then rested it on her lap. She looked at the flower printed wrapping paper with a red bow on it, then tore into it like a child opening a Christmas present.

"Wow look at that," Tyanna said as she looked over from her seat at Chyna's modelling photo that is being uncovered. Seeing her photos brought small butterflies which she felt grow, then fly around in her stomach as she looked at her younger and confident self. She smiled, then used her finger to hover over her face. She touched her unscarred nose, lips, face, then traced her beautifully curvy frame. Trey and Tyanna stood there watching Chyna, with proud smiles on their faces. Tyanna looked over at Trey, then winked at him, thanking him for doing this. She knew that this was what Chyna needed and believes that seeing her old self, will help bring back the old Chyna. Before Trey could wink back, they both heard Chyna scream, then seen the frame fly across the room and shatter as it landed on the floor.

"Chyna?" Tyanna called as she looked at her in complete shock. With his mouth wide open in shock, Trey looked at Chyna, then turned his head slowly and looked at the shattered frame resting on the floor. Before Trey could say anything, Chyna's nurse entered the room to see Chyna crying and a cracked frame on the floor.

Looking at the frame, the nurse kindly offered,

"I can come back later if you want?"

"No, it's cool," Tyanna said then rushed over to Chyna, ready to comfort her.

The nurse nodded, then reminded them all,

"I understand this is a difficult time, but you must remember that this is only temporary." Chyna ignored the nurses reassuring words and continued to cry.

"Thank you, nurse, what was it you came in here to say?" Trey asked curiously.

The nurse nodded, then told them all cheerfully,

"Doctor Lee has declared Chyna is well enough to go home. I am happy to let you all know that she has been discharged." The nurse paused then looked directly at Chyna and told her, "we will be sending out a nurse who will visit you once a week, to make sure everything is okay. The nurse will also continue to help you with your rehabilitation. We just need to add the address of where you'll be staying onto our system so we can get this setup for you." The room suddenly went silent, which told the nurse that something is up. She looked at their blank faces, then stepped back and told them before she left the room, "I'll come back later, once you've discussed everything." Tyanna looked at Trey then mouthed for him to talk to her outside.

"We'll be back in a sec," Tyanna told Chyna then left the room with Trey following. As she sat down on a chair in the corridor, Tyanna asked, "What's the plan?"

"What do you mean? She's staying at yours."

"No! She can't." Tyanna said immediately.

"Why can't she?"

Tyanna sat at the edge of her seat then told him,

"Because I live in a studio flat! There's literally not even enough space for me to move around, let alone someone with a broken leg."

"When did you move into a studio flat? Chyna told me you lived in some high-end condo." Trey told her.

Tyanna sighed then informed him,

"Unfortunately, the guy I was dealing with stopped paying for my rent once his wife found out about us. We both know I can't afford to live there, so I had to give it up." Trey shook his head disappointedly, secretly judging her a little, before he heard Tyanna ask, "what about her parents?"

Trey shook his head then told her,

"Nah, she can't. She lost contact with her parent's years ago when she moved down here. Didn't you know?" Trey noticed the blank facial expression on Tyanna's face, then decided to fill her in, "Chyna's parent's both worked until her mother got really ill, so her dad quit his job just to look after her. Chyna told me that when she was 17, she left to move in with her man at the time."

In shock, Tyanna asked,

"That's silly, why would she just leave?"

Trey shrugged then guessed,

"She didn't say but knowing Chyna I reckon it was because she wasn't getting enough attention, or she did it for a selfish reason."

"Damn... Well, I'm sure if she searches hard enough, she'll be able to find them."

"She tried when we first got together, but she couldn't find them," Trey informed her.

Tyanna sat there thinking for a few seconds before she suggested,

"Why don't you take her in?"

Trey stuttered repeatedly as he considered her suggestion.

"I would but," Trey paused, refusing to finish his sentence.

"But what? Is it that hoe Ayisha?" Tyanna said viciously.

Trey sucked his teeth agitatedly once he heard Ayisha being disrespected.

"I would but I'd have to talk to *Ayisha, my girl* first," Trey said emphasising on certain words.

"Well, what are you waiting for?" Tyanna asked before she stood up then walked off, heading back to room 101.

***

Trey pasted back and forth along the ramp outside of the hospital, battling with his thoughts. He can't believe he's even considering taking Chyna back in after he had just paid her to get out of his life for good. He reminisced on everything Chyna had done to him and those around him. From attacking Ayisha, to nearly burning down his house, to framing him. Then he remembered how supportive and forgiving Ayisha has been recently. Although they aren't together anymore, he can't help but still care for Chyna. He wants the best for her, even if that means moving back in with him. He stood still, took out his phone then called Ayisha. He holds the phone by his ear and waits for her to answer.

"Hey, how's it going down there?" Ayisha greeted him.

"It's going okay, how are you?" Trey asked as his eyes darted around the carpark.

"Good and I'm okay, I've just finished a Skype meeting with work."

"How'd that go?" Trey asked as he leans against the bricked wall.

"Not bad. They just updated me on everything that's going on down there, that's all."

"That's good," Trey paused then cleared his throat, "I've got something to ask you and whatever you say I'll go along with."

Feeling intrigued, she asked curiously,

"Why? What's up?"

Trey paused for a few seconds then said,

"They're releasing Chyna later today, but she has nowhere to stay... So, I was wondering would you be okay with Chyna staying at the house? Only for a few months until she recovers?" Ayisha froze as she registered the question in her head, in disbelief. She can't believe what she has just heard and is wondering why he has such a big heart. Secretly, she wanted to hang up the phone and tell him to call back when he had sense, but she didn't.

"Ayisha?" Trey called after not hearing a reply for a while.

"Yeah sure." Ayisha murmured feeling physically weak.

"Really?" Trey asked in complete shock.

"Yeah sure, I'll see you when you get back," Ayisha said then hung up before he could even reply.

If only:

Ayisha drove her car through the black electric gates that closed behind her. She parked in between Leroy's Range Rover and Tanya's Mini Cooper. She got out, locked her car then let herself in through the wooden double doors.

"Mother," Ayisha called as she closed the door behind her, wondering what room her parents are in.

"Hi, Ayisha," The Clarke's maid greeted her and reached out her hands, ready to take her jacket.

"Hi lovely, do you know which room my parents are in?" Ayisha asked as she handed her jacket over.

"Yes, Mr Clarke is out, but Mrs Clarke is downstairs in the cellar."

"Thank you." Ayisha smiled then walked along the glossy marble floor, heading towards the cellar.

"Mother," Ayisha called once she opened the door to the cellar. She took a step at a time, making her way down the stairs under the mansion.

"Baby girl," Tanya called joyfully once she heard Ayisha's voice.

The curved ceiling is decorated with bricks the colour of sand. The chandelier, which is positioned in the centre of the ceiling shines bright, lighting the whole room revealing shelves stocked with wines and spirits. Putting the bottle of Chardonnay back, Tanya turned around, reached out her hands ready to welcome Ayisha with a warm hug.

"How are you my darling?" Tanya asked then squeezed Ayisha once they met.

"I'm okay," Ayisha said while trying her best to hide how she is really feeling.

"That's good to hear it's nice to see you, I've missed you so much. I hardly see you now that you've moved in with Trey, how is he? How's everything going?" Tanya asked playing 21 questions. She is extremely happy and proud that Trey and Ayisha are finally together, and can't wait to have some grandbabies running around.

"Alright." Ayisha replied quietly.

Knowing that there's something wrong with Ayisha, Tanya asked,

"What's the matter sweetheart?" Ayisha sighed then walked over to the set of armchairs in the corner of the cellar, then sat down with Tanya following. "Is it Trey?" Tanya panicked unsure of what is going on.

"No, well yeah, well sort of." Ayisha answered then looked at Tanya, who is staring at her in suspense.

"What is it? Tell me." As much as Ayisha wants to get everything off her chest, she can't. The words tumble around in her mouth but won't come out.

Tanya's motherly instincts kicked in, which resulted in her guessing correctly,

"Is it Chyna?" Ayisha's eyes widened, as she wondered how her mother knew. "Tell me, sweetie, I've never seen you like this before you're scaring me." Tanya pleaded.

Ayisha nodded, then informed her,

"The same day we paid Chyna off she got into a car accident." She listened to Tanya gasp, then added, "then I found out Trey was sneaking behind my back and visiting her."

"Oh no he didn't!" Tanya yelled interrupting her, then wiggled her index finger side to side full of attitude.

"And today she moved into our spare room," Ayisha told her.

"Oh, hell no!" Tanya barked getting out of character.

"What on earth is he thinking? Who does he think he is?"

"I agreed to it." Ayisha defended Trey. Tanya gasped again then looked at Ayisha like she is crazy.

"What possessed you to do that?" Tanya confronted her.

Defending her actions, Ayisha answered,

"Because he asked me and I didn't want to say no. Mom, he's so loving and caring, you already know how he is. If I didn't see her myself, then I would have refused to let her stay with us, but once I saw her I just felt so sorry for her. She's completely different from how she was before."

Still looking at her the same way, Tanya replied,

"You agreed to let his ex move in with you?"

"Yeah… it might sound crazy, but I trust him. I really do. I know he's only doing this because he cares. It's only for a few months until she gets better."

"I don't believe this!" Tanya tutted wondering where she went wrong with Ayisha. "We both know how sneaky and psychotic Chyna is." Tanya reminded her.

"It's not as bad as it seems," Ayisha said secretly persuading herself too.

"I bet he really thinks he's the man, living with two women," Tanya said with a judgmental expression on her face.

"Mom it will be okay," Ayisha stated.

Tutting and shaking her head Tanya warned Ayisha,

"This is going to end badly mark my words."

***

Ayisha let herself into their house then closed the door behind her, to hear Trey and Chyna laughing uncontrollably and loudly. Ayisha rushed into the living room to see them both sitting comfortably on the sofa. Chyna's sitting in the corner of the sofa resting her broken leg on a pile of cushions, while Trey's sitting by her feet trying his best to draw Chyna on her cast, using a sharpie pen.

"Oh, hey baby," Trey called, then dropped the marker pen on the sofa.

"What's so funny?" Ayisha asked unimpressed.

"Look at this hun, he actually thinks this looks like me." Chyna laughed, completely forgetting about her bruised face or their part-time beef.

"I'll pass." Ayisha declined then walked past them and headed towards the kitchen, to have something strong to drink. Trey got up then followed her into the kitchen and closed the door behind him.

"Are you okay?" Trey asked in a concerned tone, as he watched her pour herself a shot of Hennessy.

"Yeah, I'm fine." Ayisha lied then gulped the shot down.

"It was just some fun, she thought I couldn't draw," Trey said justifying his actions.

"It's fine," Ayisha replied with a shrug in a weak tone.

"Okay good," Trey paused then told her, "I'm going to head over to the barbers and meet Kaleel there." He walked over to her, kissed the back of her neck, then opened the kitchen door.

***

"Yes, brother," Trey called then hugged Kaleel.

"Look at that beard." Kaleel announced, then pointed at Trey's forsaken overgrown beard. The hairs that are dangling from Trey's chin are uncombed and are different lengths. As well as his beard being overgrown, so is the hair on his head.

"Aye, leave me alone! You're just hating cause you're still praying for one." Trey teased then looked at all the other men waiting for their hairs to be cut, greeting them.

"I might not have a beard YET, but I still get the ladies." Kaleel boasted then sat back down.

"Gyal Chester." One of the men waiting to get their hair cut said, agreeing with Kaleel.

"See, he isn't hating." Kaleel laughed then heard the barber tell him

"You're up."

Kaleel walked over to the barber and sat down.

"Talking about the ladies, how's it going with you and Ayisha?" Kaleel asked as he took the apron from the barber then secured it around himself.

"It's going alright. Just been arguing lately but it's all good now." Trey told Kaleel happily.

"Argh okay, I'm shocked you're still alive to be honest. From when Ayisha turned up asking where you were, I feared that I'd never see you again." Kaleel confessed then heard everyone laugh, as they are listening to the conversation.

"Nah, we're all good trust me," Trey stated proudly.

"I hear that, have you heard anything from Chyna? Or did she really take the money and go?" Kaleel asked.

"Yeah, I spoke to her before I got here," Trey answered.

Kaleel sat up quickly then looked directly at Trey before he asked,

"Does Ayisha know?"

"Course she does, she's cool with it." Trey told them all with a massive smile on his face. Trey looked around the barbers at all the intrigued and curious eyes. From the look on their faces, he knew that he had to fill them in, so he decided to summarise his current situation.

"That same day we paid Chyna off she got into a car accident, then because of *you*," Trey paused and looked directly at Kaleel, "Ayisha found out that I wasn't at the gym, followed me and found me at the hospital with Chyna." They all laughed loudly in sync together enjoying the drama.

"My bad, what did she say?" asked Kaleel.

"She was mad as hell. Her and Tyanna got into it, I had to separate them. I told Ayisha everything and now she's cool with it,"

"She just forgave you just like that?" Kaleel asked sceptically. Before Trey could answer, one of the men waiting for their trim suggested,

"She could still be mad and secretly plotting."

Trey laughed then told them,

"Nah, trust me she's cool with it; she even agreed to Chyna moving in."

"WHAT?" One of the other men waiting shouted in disbelief.

"So, you've got your ex and your new girl living with you?" Roscoe asked.

"Yeah, he's living with his ex and his new girl." Kaleel clarified with a proud smile on his face.

"My man!" Another man who is waiting for his trim applauded Trey.

Unable to contain himself anymore, the barber finally asked,

"Are you hitting them both?" The entire barbers went silent, even the clippers were turned off. With all eyes glued onto Trey, they waited in suspense for an answer.

"Nah." Trey laughed before they all sighed disappointedly.

"If only I could get my baby mommas to live in the same house, that would be lit." The barber said then tapped Kaleel's shoulder, ready to carry on cutting his hair.

***

"Thanks, boss." Trey said confidently to the barber, as he admired his reflection that looked back at him in the mirror. His fade is perfectly blended. Like always, he has his signature curved tick cut on the left side of his hair. His border is perfectly straight, looking like it was done with a ruler. His right eyebrow has two slices at the end. His beard is perfectly cut too and dangles neatly without any hairs out of place. After tipping the barber, Trey and Kaleel decided that they were going to the gym to work out.

***

Side by side, Trey and Kaleel confidently walk into the gym. Each step that they took, the Godlier they felt.

"You might as well stop playing and just give me your number," Kaleel said to the receptionist, as he pulled out his phone and attempted to hand it over to her.

She laughed after him then stated the obvious,

"So, I see that you've finally had a trim."

They all laughed together for a few seconds until Kaleel said,

"Of course," then smoothly stroked his fresh trim with his hands.

"Very nice," she said as she watched him, "let me guess, today is your day off so you're going to work out."

"That's right," Kaleel said then tensed his muscles, "and don't think I haven't noticed you checking me out."

Trey laughed then said,

"Stop it, you're embarrassing yourself; she's just not into you like that. Obviously, if I wasn't with Ayisha then we'd be together, isn't that right?"

With the opportunity finally appearing, the receptionist wasted no time in getting the tea and asked,

"So, what exactly happened? Is Ayisha that black girl that visits from time to time?"

Trey nodded, then told her proudly,

"Yeah, that's my lady."

"Wow, you didn't waste no time in finding a replacement." She stated.

"Nah, it's not like that," Trey sniggered realising how bad this all sounded, "I've known Ayisha since I was a kid, but once Chyna started acting all crazy on me, I got rid of her and snatched Ayisha up."

"After what Chyna did to the gym, I really don't blame ya." The receptionist said whilst shaking her head.

"Done what to the gym?" Trey asked the question Kaleel wanted to ask.

"I'm sure Chyna planted those drugs that the feds found." The receptionist said. Kaleel and Trey looked at each other unsure of what to think.

"What made you say that?" Kaleel quizzed her.

"Well that same day before the feds came, she popped in asking if any of you were in, which was strange because she'd usually just walk straight past me and never say hello."

"I knew it!" Kaleel blurted out then remembered, "but I was in that day, so I should have seen her."

"Yeah, you were but you were training someone and we both know how passionate you get."

In shock, adding all the dots together, Trey said,

"Yeah, she might have come in asking for us, but that doesn't mean she had time to plant the drugs."

"I would have thought that too, but when I told her that you weren't in, she thanked me which was also strange, then went straight to the toilet... and where did they find the drugs?" The receptionist paused and waited for Trey's delayed response.

"The toilet!" Trey finally answered as he suddenly felt enraged.

"Hmm," Kaleel agreed then asked, "do we still have the recordings on CCTV?"

"No, remember the feds took everything, but I'm sure they can't do that." The receptionist moaned then watched Trey march out of the gym, without excusing himself.

***

Trey stepped into the house then slammed the door behind him, waking Chyna up from her nap. He marched into the living room, to see it is empty then turned around and started to march up the stairs. Trey stood in front of the spare room door that Chyna is occupying, then barged in refusing to knock.

"Trey?" Chyna called quietly as she woke up.

"Get the fuck out!" Trey said firmly then rushed over and dragged her up by her arms. As she felt her body being lifted, using her spare hand she shielded her stomach, then shouted in shock,

"TREY!" before she was dropped onto the carpet. As she landed on her back, her body bounced as her leg whacked off the floor. "My leg!" Chyna bawled as she felt an unbearable amount of pain travel up her leg. Chyna lay on the floor curled up like a ball trying her best to adjust her leg and ease the pain. Ignoring her cry, Trey marched over to her suitcase which is next to the wardrobe and dropped it onto its back ready to pack her stuff. "Trey my leg really hurts." Chyna called still holding onto her leg.

"Good." He shouted over her crying, then opened her suitcase.

"WHY?" Chyna yelled, "why are you doing this?"

She listened to her suitcase being unzipped, then heard him say,

"You know damn well what you did; you set me up with them drugs." From the look on Trey's face, she can tell he's livid, but the pain is too much for her to bear. She needs painkillers ASAP! As well as being in pain, being kicked out and away from

Trey is the last thing she ever wants to happen, so she did the only thing she could think of doing at the time.

"I can't breathe," Chyna stated then exaggerated on her breathing and pretended to shiver and choke.

"Chyna?" Trey panicked. He listened for her to answer but heard nothing, so he rushed over to her. "Chyna," he called again then scooped her up and rested her back onto the bed. Her eyes are 90% shut, so she can see Trey's reaction. She watches him put his hand in his pocket, which she concludes he is going to call for an ambulance, so she thought quickly and called for,

"Water," before she added in a few more coughs.

"Okay." Trey nodded then rushed towards the door.

"Pills," Chyna added with a straining effect to her voice.

Trey came charging back into the room with a glass of water and a box of painkillers. He rushed to her side, tucked his hand under her neck to hold her head up, then fed her the water. She exaggerated on the swallowing sound then asked for the painkillers.

"Here," he said quickly before he pulled a tray out of the box, popped out two painkillers then gently put them into her mouth. "Here," he repeated then held the glass close to her mouth and watched her take a big gulp and swallow them.

"Thank you," Chyna said, purposely making her voice sound faintish.

Still watching her, he said in a concerned tone,

"It's okay... are you feeling any better now?"

She added a few more coughs then said while gazing into his eyes,

"Yeah, I am now thanks."

Chyna lay there for a few more minutes just staring at Trey, enjoying having his undivided attention.

Feeling like it is the perfect time to tell him, Chyna said,

"I'm sorry."

"For what?" Trey asked completely forgetting that he was once mad at her.

"For everything," she said with their eyes still connected,

"I was just so mad at you. You treated me so badly. You forgot how down I was for you when you first told me you wanted to open the gym. I supported you 110% and then you kicked me out, all because I didn't want kids. Trey, I was so hurt and the only way for me to feel better was to make you hurt as much as I was hurting."

Trey nodded then replied,

"Yeah, you really did help me, and I've said that already... wait, did I just hear you say 'didn't'... do you still feel the same way about kids?"

She reached for his hand, held it, then told him,

"I did a lot of thinking at the hospital and trust me I was forced to, plus that was all I could do in there. We really had something special and I lost sight of what was real. All I cared about was material things... things that can be replaced and by doing that, I lost sight of something that can't be." Hearing Chyna finally apologise and hearing her hint that she would start a family, caught Trey off guard. Still holding hands, Trey and Chyna stared into each other's eyes until they heard an unexpected and firm knock on the open door.

"Oh, hey baby," Trey called, then removed his hand from Chyna's and stood up.

"What's all this?" Ayisha asked after her eyes skimmed the room and spotted an empty open suitcase on the floor, with the wardrobe doors open.

"I'll tell you about it in a sec," Trey told her, then walked over to her and greeted her with a kiss on the cheek.

"Okay," Ayisha nodded then stepped back and told him that she'd wait for him downstairs. Once she left, Trey turned back around and walked over to the suitcase on the floor.

"Do you forgive me?" Chyna asked quietly with her eyes wide open, ready to hear the answer. He zipped shut the suitcase then nodded without looking at her.

"Look at me," Chyna ordered and watched him slowly stand up, refusing to look at her. Purposely taking his time, Trey closed the wardrobe doors then turned around to face her. "Do you forgive me?" Chyna repeated herself.

"Yeah," he replied then dismissed himself, "I'm going to check on Ayisha, once I'm done, I'll bring you up something to eat."

"Okay, thank you." Chyna smiled then watched him walk out while miming 'I still love you,' to his back.

***

Ayisha's standing in front of the kitchen counter, unpacking their grocery bags.

"Hey," Trey called as he entered the kitchen.

Wasting no time and needing to know what went on upstairs between them both, Ayisha asked,

"Hey, what was all that about?" Trey walked over to the grocery bags then helped her unpack.

"I tried to kick her out," Trey told her as he took some fresh fruits out of the bag, effortlessly. He's still registering everything that Chyna had just said, in his head.

"Oh, wow why? What happened?" Ayisha asked as she stood still looking at him, holding a tin of Ackee in each hand.

"The receptionist told us that Chyna planted the drugs at the gym," Trey answered as he opened the cupboard doors.

"But we already knew that... remember when I picked you both up from the police station?" Ayisha reminded him.

"I know... just hearing what happened all over again brought back that same anger." Trey confessed then put away the tins and closed the cupboard doors.

"Oh okay, well how are you feeling now?" Ayisha asked curious to see where his head is at.

"I'm cool with it now; I'm over it. What I want to know is what's for dinner?" Trey asked as he got excited. He loves her cooking. He looks forward to seeing what new recipes she is going to try next.

"I fancy lasagne," Ayisha winked then reminded him,

"You love my lasagne." Trey clapped then started to dance loosely, swinging his body carelessly making Ayisha laugh.

"Yes! I'll leave you to it." He said then danced out of the kitchen.

Ayisha's standing in front of the counter chopping a whole onion into tiny cubes. Using her knife, she scrapes them to the side of the board next to the crushed garlic cloves. She then picks up the green bell pepper, cuts half of it, washes it, then cuts it into tiny cubes also.

*   *   *

Ayisha picked up the plate that she had dished out for Chyna and carried it upstairs into the spare room, where Chyna is. She knocked on the door then decided to let herself in.

"Aww thank you silly. You've let me into your partner's house for free, and feed me too, soon you'll be giving me Trey on a plate." Chyna said then laughed after her.

"Haha, you'd like that wouldn't you?" Ayisha said then told her, "today I've made lasagne," before she handed Chyna her plate.

"This is really good," Chyna said as she enjoyed the taste of the lasagne.

"I'm glad you like it!" Ayisha replied with a smirk on her face, as she watches her scrape the plate clean.

Chyna held out her hand then gave Ayisha the plate, while saying,

"Thanks, now be a gem and wash up my mess for me."

"You cheeky bitch!" Ayisha spat out each word passionately, then snatched the plate from her. Chyna opened her mouth with the intent to reply, but her words are slurry. Her vision began to blur, and her head suddenly felt extremely heavy.

"Not feeling too well?" Ayisha teased and watched her try her best to lift her head up. "You should have died in that crash." Ayisha wished, then smashed the plate off Chyna's head with all her strength letting out her frustration.

*   *   *

Suddenly the smell of burning oil tickled Ayisha's nostrils, waking her from her daydream.

"AHH!" She moaned then pulled the frying pan with foggy smoke floating from it off the stove. She fanned the smoke, then placed it into the sink before she turned the cold tap on. Once the cold water connected with the burning oil, a loud sizzling and a few popping sounds went off, as a cloud of smoke shot up just missing her face. She stepped back and fanned away the smoke while choking for a few seconds. She then stepped closer and turned it off.

'Get it together!' Ayisha said to herself quietly, then went to pour herself another shot of Hennessy. She took the lid off the bottle then poured herself a small portion, attempting to gulp it down, before Trey came rushing in asking her,

"Are you okay?"

"I'm fine," Ayisha said agitatedly. She gulped down her shot then firmly placed the glass onto the counter.

"What's the matter?" Trey asked then looked over to see the frying pan cooling down in the sink.

"I burnt the oil," Ayisha said, without looking at him then suggested, "let's go out to eat."

He watched her turn around to face him, then voiced,

"But I want your Lasagne."

"We can go to an Italian restaurant," Ayisha said then turned back around and put the Hennessy bottle away.

Spotting the Hennessy bottle, Trey smirked then said,

"Oh, I see," before he stepped closer to her and placed his hands on her hips, "you want dinner then some dessert."

"Yeah, something like that," Ayisha said while forcing out a smile.

"We can skip dinner and get straight to dessert," Trey suggested then heard Ayisha say,

"Nuh uh, I'm actually hungry, come on let's get ready," as she stepped out of his embrace. She reached for his arm, then pulled him out of the kitchen.

Ayisha's standing in front of the mirror on the wardrobe door, looking at her reflection. She is wearing a long black dress that hugs her small curves, and a pair of open-toe black heels to match. Her short, perfectly cut, bob is freshly straightened and sits in position without any hair strands out of place. Wanting to try something new and experiment with her look a little, she combed some hair to the side, placed it behind her ear, then secured it with a few bobby pins. Liking the new change and feeling good within herself, she decided to make even more of an effort. She retrieves her pink, Fenty lip gloss and applies a coating onto her lips. She rubs her lips together, then blew a kiss at herself in the mirror feeling slightly conceited. She then took a step back just to get one last good look at herself. She admires her mocha brown skin, that glistens from using her favourite body lotion. Feeling completely satisfied with her look and not wanting Trey to wait on her, she turns around and picks up her silky black clutch bag and places the silver chain strap over her shoulder. Remembering her phone that she had put on charge before she even started to get ready, she walks over and unplugged it from the charger then left their room.

As Ayisha closed their bedroom door, she heard Chyna say,

"Oh, wow you look nice," with a hint of jealousy in her voice. Seeing Ayisha leave the room that she once slept in brought back a mixture of emotions. Plus seeing Ayisha all dolled up and ready to go on a date with Trey angered her inside.

From being startled by Chyna, Ayisha laughed then replied,

"Oh, thank you."

"Where are you off to?" Chyna enquired as she rested comfortably on her crutches.

"Just going out to get something to eat," Ayisha answered then said boastfully, "we fancy some Italian food. We don't know what time we'll get back so don't wait up," before she winked, then walked past her and stood at the top of the stairs.

"Don't worry I won't!" Chyna barked then flipped her middle finger up to Ayisha's back before Ayisha headed downstairs. *"Bitch,"* Chyna muttered under her breath then went to use the toilet.

"Look at you," Trey called as he watched Ayisha enter the living room, adoring her.

"Thank you," Ayisha said as she walked over to him.

"Well damn!" Trey whistled, "I haven't seen those babies in a while." Trey added as his eyes focused on her chest.

She giggled in embarrassment then moaned,

"I know right, they keep growing."

"I'm not complaining!" Trey said then pulled her close.

"Okay, come on now before we miss our reservation," Ayisha said as she stepped out of his embrace and headed to the front door.

***

Trey pulled out the seat from under the table, waited for Ayisha to sit down, then pushed it in for her.

"Thank you," Ayisha smiled then felt him peck her neck.

"No problem beautiful," Trey replied as he walked around the waiter and sat down on the chair opposite her.

"Would you like the drinks menu before you order?" The waiter offered as he prepared to hand them one each.

"Okay, but I already know what I want to eat!" Ayisha snapped. Immediately, Trey looked at her subliminally telling her that was rude. Understanding that her statement came across too strong, Ayisha apologised then took the menu off the waiter,

"Sorry, it's just that I'm starving."

"Alright, what would you like?" The waiter asked Ayisha while he pulled out his mini note pad and pen from his trouser pocket.

"I'd like the Focaccia and the Lasagne Bolognese with garlic bread and salad."

The waiter looked up from his note pad then warned Ayisha,

"The Focaccia is a light Italian bread with rosemary, it's quite similar to garlic bread, do you still want them both?"

"Hmm, it's okay, scrap that I just want the garlic bread," Ayisha answered, then heard Trey have the audacity to say,

"We can always get that bread for Chyna." Ayisha looked at Trey evilly; if looks could kill he would have died right there on the spot. She squinted her eyes then said,

"We're out on a date, I really don't want to hear anything about that woman right now."

"But she needs something to eat, I forgot to bring her up something," Trey argued his point across calmly, knowing that was best. Considering the mood Ayisha is in right now, he figured that she might just bite his head off.

"She can get the leftovers." Ayisha snapped with that same evil look on her face.

Trey laughed awkwardly then replied,

"We can't do that."

"Oh, yes we can!" Ayisha told Trey, then heard the waiter say,

"I'll just come back in a few minutes," before he put his note pad and pen away.

"Trey I'm dead serious right now, I really don't know why you're playing with me! We're out spending quality time together and you're sitting here worrying about her." Ayisha said furiously.

"Ayisha, you're sounding crazy right now she's got to eat."

Ayisha rolled her eyes then suggested,

"We can stop off at the petrol station on the way back and get her a sandwich."

"But why? We're at a nice restaurant it only takes 2 to 3 minutes to order an extra meal and carry it home."

"Trey! I couldn't care less if that girl eats right now, so it's either a cold sandwich from the shop or nothing at all!" Ayisha offered. From the look in Ayisha's eyes, he can tell that she is getting annoyed which he found ridiculous, but then he remembered what little time alone they've had, since taking Chyna in.

Trey shook his head then said,

"Okay, you're right," before he turned around and looked for the waiter.

"Thank you and I'm really sorry about earlier." Ayisha apologised as she handed the same waiter the drinks menu.

"It's okay when you've got to eat, then I guess you've got to eat." The waiter shrugged feeling philosophical, "I'll make sure you don't wait too long for your food."

"Aww thank you and I hope not, or else I'll burst into that kitchen and cook the food myself." Ayisha teased. The waiter chuckled for a few seconds then took Trey's menu.

"Well, someone is hungry." Trey laughed then heard Ayisha say,

"Yeah I really am," before she poured them both some icy cold water.

"Just look at those babies," Trey said as he stared at her chest.

"Oh my gosh, stop it!" Ayisha chuckled then covered them with her hands. "They've been getting so big lately, I really don't like them."

"Oh, I do!" Trey told her still with his eyes glued to her chest, "I'll show you how much later." Trey said before the waiter cleared his throat, then rested a basket of warm bread onto their table.

"Thank you." Ayisha laughed awkwardly, knowing that he had heard what Trey said.

"See isn't this nice? Just the two of us together spending quality time, like what normal couples do." Ayisha said while playing footsie under the table with him.

"It always is," Trey said completely missing her point.

"We haven't had time alone in so long! It's literally like we're parents. But instead of looking after a baby, we're taking care of a grown ass woman."

Trey laughed then agreed,

"That's true but remember it won't be forever."

"Oh, I know that, and I can't wait." She replied then felt her mouth suddenly fill up with saliva. "Can you smell that?" Ayisha asked in disgust as the smell of warm garlic entered her nostrils.

The waiter's standing by Ayisha with a proud smile on his face. He is proud that he was able to deliver their food, within such a short period of time, so they didn't have to wait that long. Still smiling, he placed the lasagne, salad and garlic bread onto the table in front of Ayisha, which resulted in her covering her mouth and nose with her hands. "That smells." Ayisha blurted out from behind her hands, as her eyes examined the plate.

"What are you on about?" Trey asked as he looked at her like she is crazy.

"It smells," Ayisha repeated herself, then pushed the plate away from her and stood up. The waiter stood there looking at Ayisha with a confused look on his face, unsure of how to react or what to say.

"Ayisha, what's wrong with you? There's nothing wrong with it." Trey stated as he looked up at her with a confused look on his face also. Feeling her stomach turn even more due to the smell, Ayisha ignored their confused glances and ran to the ladies' room.

"I'm really not sure what to say, it smells and looks perfectly fine to me," Trey reassured the waiter.

"Yeah." The waiter shrugged, still standing there in shock.

"I guess you should just put our food in a takeaway box," Trey suggested, then watched the waiter sigh heavily. "My bad, don't worry I'll sort you out," Trey added, then took his wallet out and tipped him $30. "Can you please bring the bill and I'll go check on her quickly," Trey said. A smile grew across the waiter's face as he folded his tip and slipped it into his pocket.

"Thanks man." The waiter said before Trey left the table. He gently tapped on the ladies' bathroom door, then called for Ayisha before he placed his ear close to the door listening for a reply.

"Come in," Ayisha said then opened the door for him. He stepped into the bathroom then closed the door behind him.

"Are you okay?" Trey asked then walked over and began to comfort her.

"No, I'm so embarrassed," Ayisha confessed then began to cry.

"Hey, hey, where's all this coming from? What's wrong?" Trey asked as he wiped away her tears. She ignored him and carried on crying. She is aware that she was acting silly, but for some reason, she just couldn't stop crying. "Do you want to go home?" Trey suggested then felt her nod on his chest.

"Yeah," Ayisha replied then cried even harder.

"It's okay," Trey said then carried on comforting her. She hugged him back, then sighed heavily feeling calmer and 100% safe in his arms. "We'll go home in a few minutes; I've just got to pay for our food first. Are you okay now?" He asked while stroking her hair, not wanting to leave her until he knew that she was okay.

"Yeah." She sniffled then let him go.

"Okay, I won't be long," Trey reassured her then walked to the door. He pressed down on the handle and was about to open it until he heard Ayisha call him. "Yeah?" Trey answered as he looked back at her. She wiped away her tears, smiled then told him while looking deep into his eyes,

"I love you." Hearing this made a massive smile grow across his face.

"I love you too," He said back then opened the door and went to collect their food, forgetting to get Chyna something to eat.

Trip down memory lane:

Ayisha lay in bed under the covers trying her best to fall asleep but she couldn't. She is still embarrassed by her random and emotional outburst last night. Every time her eyes would close, she would replay the same scene in her mind, then once she would open her eyes, she would feel that same embarrassing and confused feelings all over again. Suddenly Ayisha felt the mattress wobble, which felt like the third time within a minute, which told her that Trey couldn't sleep either. Laying on her back, she looked over to her side to face him, then asked,

"Can't you sleep either?"

"I've been trying too," Trey confessed then tossed over to lay on his side, so that he could look at her. "I keep thinking about what happened last night." Ayisha sighed dreadfully, then tossed over on her side to face him. "I wanted to speak to you about it once we got back, but you went straight to bed."

"I know, I just wanted the day to finish already. I was so embarrassed."

Trey nodded sympathetically, then asked,

"What happened yesterday? What was that all about?"

Feeling the same emotions resurface again, Ayisha sighed, then answered back untruthfully,

"I don't know." She figured that it was best for her not to tell him, mainly due to her not knowing the exact reason for her outburst, but she thought it might have something to do with the complicated situation they are currently in with Chyna.

"Are you sure?" Trey asked sceptically.

"I'm sure," She lied then reached for the side of his face and stroked it with her hand.

"Okay," he said slowly as he gazed into her eyes, "oh wait, I recall someone finally telling me they love me yesterday."

She giggled then replied,

"I think you heard wrong."

"Oh, is that so?" Trey laughed then pounced up and started to tickle her.

"Get off me!" She laughed uncontrollably, as she tried her best to push his hands away from her.

"Don't run now." Trey laughed before he felt himself being kicked off the bed.

"Didn't expect that did you?" Ayisha teased, then crawled to the end of the bed and scuffled his hair as he sat there in shock.

"Argh, come on not my hair." Trey laughed then pushed her hand away. She joined in laughing then stood up on the bed victoriously as she flexed her arms, showing off her tiny muscles.

"Don't underestimate my strength." Ayisha teased then heard him say,

"I won't," before he stood up to his feet and felt her muscles. "But they haven't got anything on mine," Trey said as he flexed his.

"Oh whatever," Ayisha laughed then stepped down off the bed and began to make it while she asked, "what have you got planned for today then, Mr muscles?"

"I'm hitting the gym," Trey answered as he helped her make the bed.

"Good! Cause you weren't hard to take down." Ayisha teased then winked at him.

***

Trey entered the gym to see the receptionist look up from her desk then quickly look away. She's unsure what to expect, because the last time she saw him, was when he marched out of the gym angrily because of what she said. Plus, she really loves working there, so she doesn't want to give him any reason to get rid of her. Trey walked over to the desk, then leant on it whilst smiling at her.

"Hey, how are you?" He asked as he watched her slowly look up at him.

"I'm fine thanks, how about yourself?" She asked still on edge.

"I'm good, thanks for letting me know about the whole drugs situation. All is forgiven." He told her then took a bar of chocolate out of his hooded jacket. He slowly handed it over to her, then asked, "are we still friends?" She started laughing uncontrollably, then took the bar of chocolate off him while saying,

"Hell yeah!" before she ripped it open and offered him some.

"Thanks," he winked then broke a row off and bit into it.

"What's the numbers looking like today?" Trey asked with his mouth full. She filled her mouth with as much chocolate as she could, then checked the computer. After swallowing what was in her mouth, she informed him,

"Two people have joined today *so far,* and we had a few calls inquiring about joining."

"That's lower than usual," Trey stated in a disappointed tone.

"It's still early we'll get more later on. People are still in bed."

"I hope so, where's Kaleel?" Trey asked.

"He's just showing one of the new members around, he should be done soon. He's got one more to show around after."

She answered, then pointed at a dark-skinned bald chubby man. Suddenly, Trey felt a frog in his throat once he spotted the chubby man's face. He stood there staring at the familiar face, trying his best to remember his name, but he couldn't.

"Trey," Kaleel called from behind him. Being startled, Trey turned around then greeted Kaleel with a hug.

"What's good?" Trey asked Kaleel with his mind elsewhere. It irritated him that he couldn't think of the familiar face's name.

"I'm good, just finished showing Mr Fitzbert around," Kaleel answered.

"Nice, welcome," Trey said to Mr Fitzbert then shook his hand.

"Trey owns the gym," Kaleel told Mr Fitzbert.

"Nice place you have here. It's good to see that a black man owns it." Mr Fitzbert said proudly.

"Thanks, I appreciate it." Trey replied, then looked around the gym with his eyes reminding himself of how far he has come in life.

"Well, I'm going to change into my gym clothes, it was nice meeting you." Mr Fitzbert said then made his way towards the changing room.

"Remember, if you ever need a personal trainer then I'm here." Kaleel reminded him then said to Trey, "I'm just going to show that guy around, then I'll come chill for a bit."

"Yeah man, that's cool," Trey nodded then watched Kaleel walk over to the waiting area and introduce himself to the familiar face. He watched him struggle to stand up to shake Kaleel's hand.

"I'm just going to show you around the gym and give you a brief introduction on how to use the machines." Trey heard Kaleel say. The familiar face nodded, showing Kaleel that he understood, then started to waddle towards Trey. He swallowed his spit, nervously and smiled at Trey. Not recognising him, he forced out a smile then looked past Trey at all the equipment that is available. Concluding that he doesn't recognise him, Trey turned around then asked the receptionist,

"What's the name of that bald man Kaleel's showing around?"

"Hmm... Collin?" The receptionist guessed, then moved the mouse around while making a few clicking sounds, as she looked for the contact details of their new members. "His name is..." The receptionist paused then read out loud, "Terry Hudson."

"Terry Hudson," Trey echoed slowly, digesting the name. He suddenly felt a bundle of mixed emotions begin to resurface, as he reminisced on the role that Terry played in his life and the day he randomly left.

***

Trey hung around in the waiting area patiently waiting for Kaleel to finish showing Terry around. As he waited, he went over in his head repeatedly what he was going to say to him.

"Thanks for showing me around." Terry thanked Kaleel as he struggled to catch his breath. Just by walking around the gym tired him out. With sweat resting on the surface of his forehead and his neck, he shook Kaleel's hand then, listened to Kaleel say,

"No problem, I look forward to our first session on Thursday." Trey stood up, then walked over to them by the desk.

"Terry this is Trey, the owner of the gym." Kaleel introduced them to each other. Hearing the name rang a bell in Terry's head. He looked into Trey's eyes as he mouthed,

"Trey?"

"Yeah, it's been a while," Trey answered then took a good look at him. He looked at Terry's chubby arms, then at his belly which is round and hanging over his trousers, then at his double chin that dangles in front of his neck then at his bald head which is covered with sweat. He looks like a completely different person to how Trey remembered him all those years ago. He has completely let himself go.

"You look well," Terry said sincerely before he gasped for his breath.

"Thanks," Trey replied, then stopped himself from lying and saying the same thing back. He planned on confronting Terry and imagined him battering him black and blue for breaking Claire's heart, but he couldn't.

"I take it you two know each other," Kaleel said as he looked at them both.

"Yeah, we do. This is the man that walked out on me and Ma and broke her heart." Trey said bitterly.

Terry bowed his head feeling embarrassed then said,

"I'm really sorry. I was selfish back then. I wasn't mentally fit enough to be a husband let alone take on the role of being somebody's dad."

"Yeah, I know," Trey paused then clutched his fist, "how any man can just walk out on their family blows my mind. You weren't a man then you were a boy!"

Agreeing with him, Terry nodded then answered,

"You're right son. I wasn't. I was selfish back then and I've only just realised this, at the age of 50." Trey nodded but refused to say anything back. As angry as he is at Terry, he stopped his urges and ignored his inner thoughts of kicking him out or beating his ass. Even though it was so late Trey appreciated the apology and understood that he is finally sorting his life out, even if it is more than 19 years later. "How's your mom? How is Claire doing?" Terry asked curiously.

"She's great! She'll never need for nothing because I take care of her! I stepped up and became the man she needed in her life." Trey said passionately.

"Good, you're more of a man then I will ever be." Terry applauded Trey.

"I know!" Trey nodded then calmed himself down, before he walked over to the desk. Hearing everything and watching from the corner of her eye, the receptionist looked down at her desk and began to type randomly on the keyboard.

"Hey beautiful, please print a free pass for Mr Hudson," Trey ordered calmly.

"Of course." She said then began to click away.

Trey turned around to look at Kaleel and Terry then said,

"There's no bad blood on my side. You're more than welcome to use the gym whenever you want. All I ask is that you don't contact Claire." Terry nodded then thanked Trey gratefully. "No problem, I'll see you both another time," Trey said then hugged Kaleel and left.

As he left the building, Trey pulled out his keys and made his way over to his car. He unlocked it, got in and called Claire. He listened to it ring a few times, then heard her answer,

"Hi baby, how are you?"

"I'm good Ma, how are you?"

"That's good. I'm just out doing some food shopping. Where are you? At the gym?" Claire guessed knowing her son so well.

"Yeah," he answered then requested, "can you stop by mine later?"

"Of course, sweetie. Once I've finished off here then I'll stop by straight after." Claire told him before she blew a kiss through the phone then hung up.

* * *

Trey and Ayisha are sitting on the sofa cuddling with Chyna sitting at the end watching American Gangster, all for the first time.

"I've got to pee again." Chyna said as she struggled to get up and use her crutches.

"It's probably those pain killers they've got you on." Trey guessed.

"It could be," Chyna said then hopped along on her crutches to use the downstairs toilet.

A gentle knock on the front door distracted Trey and Ayisha from watching the film.

"That should be Claire," Trey told Ayisha, then got up and rushed to the door not wanting her to be waiting for too long. He looked through the peephole to see Claire standing outside, holding onto a brown paper grocery bag, full of fruits, vegetables and water. He opened the door and watched her step inside.

"Hi, sweetie pie." Claire greeted him, then stepped out of their hug and handed him the bag, "I thought I'd buy you some stuff too."

"Thanks, Ma." Trey smiled then carried the bag into the living room while Claire closed the door.

"Where's my daughter in law?" Claire asked as she walked into the living room and spotted Ayisha sitting on the sofa. "Hi sweetie, how are you?" she asked then rushed over to hug her.

"Hey, I'm fine thanks, we're just watching a film," Ayisha answered as they hugged.

"Aww look at you two," Claire said admiring them being together before she sat down beside her.

"Ma, do you want some tea or coffee?" Trey called from the kitchen, knowing his mother very well.

"Oh, yes please, I'll have some tea today," Claire shouted back, then pulled her leather gloves off her hands until the sound of Chyna's crutches hitting off the wooden floorboards startled her. She looked over to the living room door, where the increasing noise was coming from then spotted Chyna enter the living room. She gasped loudly as she stared at Chyna like she had just seen a ghost. Spotting Claire, Chyna stood still and balanced on her crutches. Not wanting Claire to see her face, she hid her fading scars behind her hands.

"Take me upstairs," Chyna demanded as she began to shake and panic.

"What on earth?" Claire mumbled not believing her eyes. Chyna was the last person Claire expected to see here and from what she understood, Chyna took the money and should've been anywhere else but here. Hearing Chyna panic, Trey dropped the sugar onto the kitchen counter then darted into the living room. "Trey, what's this?" Claire questioned him in a confused and disappointed tone.

"I'll explain after I bring her upstairs," Trey answered then rushed to Chyna's side. Knowing that Claire and Trey needed to have a mother and son talk, Ayisha stood up and offered to take Chyna upstairs.

"Yes, let her!" Claire demanded bluntly, then gave Trey 'the look' that told him they needed to talk. Trey swallowed his spit, then slowly took Chyna's crutches from her and rested them on the armrest of the sofa.

"Once I'm done, I'll stay upstairs," Ayisha told them, then walked over to Chyna and placed her arm around her shoulder and helped her leave the room. Not even waiting for them both to leave, Claire asked Trey,

"What on earth is going on here? Why is that psychopath in this house?" Struggling to balance and knowing that it would take her forever to turn around, Chyna looked over her shoulder and confronted Claire,

"Who are you calling a psycho?" Chyna barked.

"Behave yourself!" Ayisha said then sped up to remove Chyna out of the room even quicker.

"Yeah, you better hop away or else I'll break your other leg!" Claire barked back as she pointed at Chyna with her index finger.

"You're lucky she's dragging me away!" Chyna yelled. Not allowing his mother to be disrespected, Trey pointed at Chyna then warned her,

"Watch your mouth!"

"She started it," Chyna stated as she is being escorted away.

"How dare she disrespect me like that! Why is she even here Trey?" Claire played 21 questions.

Trey sat down next to her dreading the conversation they are about to have. Realising that he is sitting too close to Claire, within reaching distance, he moved away from her on the sofa before he explained,

"The same day we paid Chyna off, she got into a car accident and because she was still on my insurance, they called me, so I went to visit her which I kept doing until Ayisha found out."

Interrupting him, Claire asked,

"What did Ayisha say? I guess she wasn't mad because look at you all, playing open house."

"She was mad at first but she's okay about it now," Trey answered then watched Claire shake her head.

"You and Ayisha have lost your damn minds. To think I approved of Ayisha." Claire said in disgust.

"Ma, it's not as bad as it seems. Chyna needed somewhere to stay so we took her in. It's only for a couple of months until she gets better." Trey defended their actions.

"I can't believe Ayisha agreed to all of this... wait... are you guys living in some sick fantasy world? Are you getting your cake and eating it too?" Claire asked with her face still screwed up in disgust.

"No, why does everyone think that?"

"Because that's what it sounds like... I'm still trying to figure out what was going on in your minds when you took that psycho home." Claire said, baffled.

"She was vulnerable and scared. She really needed someone to be there with her and we felt sorry for her."

"Trey, she got what she deserved. She ruined your life and tried to tarnish everything you had worked so hard on building, not to mention, she was the reason why you were arrested... God knows how hard I worked on preventing that ever happening to you."

"I know... but she's changed," Trey stated then heard Claire start to laugh.

"Wait, were you just there when she disrespected me? She definitely seems like a changed person." Claire said sarcastically.

"I did, and I'll speak to her later."

Claire sighed, then told him calmly,

"Son, I dislike the decisions you've been making. It seems like Chyna has you under her spell and I don't like it! You've got the girl you've always wanted ever since you were a boy, but instead your stuck on rotten goods," she paused and thought of something, "I want Chyna out of here by the end of the month, if she's not gone by then I will remove her myself. Do I make myself clear?" He heard what Claire had just said but refused to say anything. "Trey do I make myself clear?" Claire asked again. Still not hearing a response, she moved closer to Trey, grabbed his hand then begged, "Son, you've finally got Ayisha and I'm so happy for you, only God knows how much I am. But I'm begging you, please, please, please, don't ruin this. Women like Ayisha, are very rare and I can guarantee you won't find someone like her again." He nodded. "I bet she's secretly not okay with all of this. I'm guessing that she only went along with the idea just to make you happy." Claire guessed.

"You think so?" Trey asked, then replayed Ayisha's reaction's in his head, "I think your right Ma. The other day when we were eating out, Ayisha lost it once I mentioned Chyna's name."

"There you go! I know how much she really means to you and I know that you don't want to lose her. Shoot, I don't want you to lose her either! So, I think you should do something special for her, just to show her how much she is appreciated." Claire suggested.

"Okay, I will, because she really does deserve it." Trey smiled, then leant forward and kissed Claire on her cheek.

"You're welcome son, now where is my tea?" Claire laughed then watched him stand up and make his way to the kitchen.

He re-entered the living room carrying two cups of tea over to the sofa. Hearing Trey's footsteps getting closer, Claire sat forward then re-positioned the mats, ready for Trey to rest their cups onto them.

"Thank you, son," Claire said then took one of the teacups off him.

"You're welcome." He replied then sat down next to her.

"Was Chyna the reason why you called me over?"

"Oh no, well yeah, but not just for that."

Claire sipped on her tea then asked,

"What was it then?"

Trey cleared his throat, then said slowly but clearly,

"I saw Terry at the gym today." She froze for a few seconds as she registered the name she had erased from her memory, then took another sip of her tea. "He asked about you and I told him that you're doing good without him and warned him not to contact you," Trey informed her. Claire nodded slowly, then looked into her cup and swirled the tea around, controlling her emotions. As angry as she is, she can't help but wonder, so she asks,

"How is he?" Unable to hold it back anymore, Trey laughed uncontrollably as he told her,

"I remember him being a chubby guy back then, but now he's obese."

"Obese?" Claire echoed then joined in the laughter, "I take it he moved in with his mother after all! I really despise that woman. All she ever does is smother him and treat him like a baby."

"You can tell because he's a big guy now," Trey said whilst still laughing. "Literally."

"To think he still lives down here."

"I thought the same thing." Trey agreed.

After Claire left, Trey met up with Kaleel and they spent a few hours looking for something to buy for Ayisha. After looking at clothes and accessories for a while, they both decided it was best to buy her some jewellery, which they wished that they thought of first.

* * *

Trey let himself into the house then closed the door behind him.

"Ayisha," He called in an excited tone, then headed to the living room.

"Hey," Ayisha said as she sat up on the sofa.

"Hey Chy," Trey called after he kissed Ayisha. Chyna huffed and puffed under her breath, once she saw their lips connect, then smiled at Trey once she spotted the gift bag he is holding.

"What's in the bag?" Chyna asked as she stared at the white bag with pink polka dots on.

"This is for you baby," Trey told Ayisha, then rested the gift bag on her lap with a proud smile on his face. Unlike Chyna, Ayisha doesn't expect gifts.

"Oh, thank you," Ayisha said in shock, then looked at the bag curiously. Chyna's sitting on the end of the sofa with her legs resting on a mountain of cushions, watching Ayisha with eyes full of envy.

"Well open it then!" Chyna demanded in a rude tone before she rolled her eyes.

"Yeah, open it," Trey agreed as he stood over her watching. Ayisha nodded, then opened the gift bag and pulled out a navy rectangular box with a bow on. She removed the lid with the bow to discover a diamond encrusted bracelet with an emerald on. Chyna growled under her breath as she watched, hating the fact that Ayisha is now the one receiving his gifts. "It came with matching earrings," Trey told her proudly.

"Thanks, but why did you buy this?" Ayisha asked gratefully but confused.

"You never ask why you just accept them," Chyna said in an agitated tone. Ayisha ignored Chyna, then reached for Trey's hand and kissed it.

"There's more." He told her, then watched her look into the bag and pull out another jewellery box. She opened it to see a matching pair of stud earrings.

"Aww thank you," Ayisha said, as Trey watched her close the box and place it on the sofa by her leg, which made his smile disappear. He is so used to Chyna trying on whatever he had brought straight away, that seeing her gifts being put straight down upset him.

"There's more." Trey managed to say before he heard Chyna say in shock,

"More!"

Ayisha ignored Chyna, then reached into the bottom of the bag and pulled out a small ring size box. Once Chyna spotted it, her jaw dropped as her heart shattered into a thousand pieces. She's 100% sure she knows what is inside. She then began to reminisce on the day Trey proposed to her, by finding the ring in the bottom of her wine glass. Ayisha slowly opened the box, fearing to see what is inside. As the lid was lifted, she spotted an 18ct white gold diamond ring. Ayisha gasped with one hand holding the box and the over covering her mouth. He laughed at her reaction, then took the box off her and removed the ring. He knelt on one knee in front of her, pulled her right hand that is covering her mouth, then said,

"This is a thank you for everything because I really appreciate you and everything you do."

"Oh, so, this isn't an engagement ring?" Ayisha asked desperately needing clarification.

"Oh, no," he laughed, "well not for now, it's just a promise ring," Trey said then slid the ring onto her finger. Chyna exhaled in relief, then looked at her own engagement ring. She smiled at it, admiring the diamond, then raised her hand positioning it so Ayisha could see then boasted,

"Your ring's nice but it isn't as big as mine." Feeling the metal securely wrapped around her finger, reassured Ayisha of how Trey feels for her. Having this ring, meant that he is serious about their relationship and it will eventually lead to marriage. Feeling empowered, Ayisha sucked her teeth then told Trey,

"I think it's about time you take back that ring, it's not even like you're engaged anymore." Still on one knee, Trey looked at Ayisha questioning if she is serious or not. "Yeah, I think it's something that needs to be done and hopefully this will kick her off her pedestal because she keeps trying me!"

"I think the fuck not," Chyna said bluntly.

Ayisha looked at Trey seriously, then told him to,

"Go and get it." He nodded then stood up and took a few steps along the sofa towards Chyna. She tried to move, but her legs restricted her, so he reached for her hand and tried to grab it, but she quickly crossed her arms.

"Chyna stop acting like a brat," Trey said in a fed-up tone.

"Why? You used to love it before," Chyna reminded him which triggered something inside of Ayisha. She pushed the bag and gifts off her lap, as she muttered,

"I've had enough," then got up and charged over to them. "Move Trey!" Ayisha demanded, then moved him to the side and stood over her on the sofa. "You're going to give me that ring! It's not like you can run away," Ayisha demanded as she gritted her teeth. She reached for Chyna's arms then yanked them so they were unfolded. With her eyes completely focused on Chyna's engagement ring, Ayisha let go, then grabbed hold of Chyna's right arm and attempted to reach for it, until Chyna shaped her hand into a fist making it even more difficult for Ayisha to get. "Loosen your hand!" Ayisha demanded still with her teeth gritted, then watched Chyna smirk at her.

"Chyna, stop," Trey said as he watched.

"No, it's mine," Chyna shouted keeping her hand shaped into a fist. With Ayisha's blood above boiling point, she used her nails to pinch Chyna's flesh as hard as she could. "Argh!" Chyna bellowed as Trey said to Ayisha,

"Calm down." He stood there watching helplessly. This wasn't the first time he had seen them nearly bite each other's heads off and he didn't want to see it happen again. Not wanting there to be a repeat of what happened outside of the hub, he leant forward and tried to pull Ayisha away.

"Trey, just go!" Ayisha commanded as she wiggled out of his grip, still pinching into Chyna's skin.

"You're hurting me." Chyna yelled at the top of her lungs, then leant forward and took a huge bite into Ayisha's hand.

"Argh!" Ayisha bellowed then used her spare hand to slap Chyna's face. Hearing the connection of Ayisha's palm hit her cheek and feeling her bruises and scars being slapped shocked Chyna. Trey stood there staring at Ayisha gobsmacked. He can still hear the sound of Chyna's cheek being slapped echo in his head. Still holding her cheek, Chyna loosened her hand slowly which Ayisha spotted, so she grabbed Chyna's hand and pulled the ring off her finger. Ayisha held the ring in the air victoriously like it was a trophy, then stepped down from the sofa and handed it to Trey. He slowly took the ring off Ayisha, then watched her calmly walk over to the gifts and put them into the bag, like everything was fine. Chyna looked up at Trey, while still holding onto her cheek that sizzled and waited for him to comfort her, but he didn't. Instead, he followed Ayisha out of the living room with an impressed smirk on his face.

But who?

The clock displayed 3:58 am before the screen on Ayisha's phone lit up, as it started to ring. Hearing the unexpected annoying ringing sound go off, woke Ayisha and Trey up. Ayisha mumbled as she forced herself to move and answer her phone.

"Hello?" Ayisha greeted the person on the other line, in a half-asleep tone, as she struggled to see out of her tired eyes. She forced herself to sit up then listened carefully before she suggested, "can't Bruno do it?" She listened for a few more seconds, nodded, then said, "okay, I'm coming." *'Coming?'* Trey repeated in his head as he listened. Ayisha ended the call, then rubbed her eyes having no energy whatsoever.

"Where are you going?" Trey asked as he looked at her.

"Back to LA," Ayisha answered, then yawned and stretched at the same time.

"Why?"

"Work has a really big project on, and they need me to fly out and help them."

"But I thought they were okay with you working from down here?" Trey said.

"They are, but they really need me. They've even offered to reimburse my travel expenses, so I know how desperate they are." Trey moaned not wanting her to leave. He planned on sitting Ayisha and Chyna down to discuss what happened last night, with the hope of getting rid of all the tension in the house.

"Can you pass me the Mac?" Ayisha asked then pointed at the MacBook on the table next to his bedside.

He reached for the Mac then handed it to her before he suggested,

"Can't you just go later?"

"No, I can't. But it should only be for a few days." Ayisha guessed then opened the Mac and began to search for flights from Houston to Los Angeles.

"But who's going to get Chyna ready?"

"I don't know, but one thing I do is it won't be you!" Ayisha said in a serious tone. "Call the hospital and get them to send out a carer or someone that can help you out until I'm back."

Trey listened to her suggestion then pleaded,

"Don't go," before he stroked her arm.

"I've got too but I'll be back soon."

***

It is 8:05 am and Trey and Ayisha have just finished packing her belongings. Trey walked ahead of Ayisha rolling her suitcase along the corridor, then down the stairs towards the car.

"It's not too late to cancel your flight," Trey suggested playfully as he stood in front of the door.

She laughed then reminded him,

"It's only for a few days," as she unlatched the front door then slowly opened it.

"Aren't you forgetting something?" Trey hinted. He watched her think for a few seconds, then pulled her keys out from his pocket and dangled it in the air.

"Oh my gosh, give it here!" She chuckled then jumped up and down trying to get them.

He laughed then repeated,

"It's not too late to cancel your flight."

"Trey stop it, the time will fly by." Ayisha said then pulled his arm down and took the keys off him. He followed Ayisha outside out of the house, with her black and purple suitcase trailing behind them. He watched her press the button for her trunk to open then placed it inside, closed it, then pulled her close.

"Text me once you've got there," Trey said then hugged her.

"I will," Ayisha promised then rested her head against his chest. They stood there hugging for a while until Ayisha remembered her flight.

"I've got to go," Ayisha said then stepped out of his hug.

"Okay, love you,"

"I love you too," Ayisha replied before kissing him. He watched her get into the car and put on her seatbelt. She waved at him before she reversed off their drive which pulled a string on Trey's heart. He waved then watched her drive off. He stood there sadly, just staring into the distance where Ayisha's car had disappeared, already missing her.

After a few more minutes, Trey re-entered the house then made his way into the kitchen and switched on the kettle. Missing Ayisha, he rested on the counter feeling sorry for himself until his phone received a text. He unlocked it to read a message from the hospital, informing him that they have received his text and that a carer should arrive for 9 am. He placed his phone onto the counter then looked around the kitchen. His eyes spotted some dishes in the sink, and their dustbin that is overflowing. Not wanting the carer to think they are messy people, Trey walked over to the bin, removed the bag and tied it, forgetting to double it up by putting it into another bag. Trey carried the bag over to the outdoor bin and dropped it onto the floor. He lifted the lid and held it open, then quickly picked up the bin bag, not wanting the lid to shut close. He tried to drop the bag into the bin before the lid shut, but instead, it hit off the corner of the bin, which resulted in it popping and the rubbish falling out of the bag. He sucked his teeth, then dropped the bag on the floor before he went back inside to get another bag. He carried it outside, opened it then began to pick everything up and transfer them into the new bag. He picked up Ayisha's empty lotion container then gazed at it. He smiled for a few seconds as it reminded him of her. Pulling himself back together, he dropped the container into the bag then looked at the rest of the mess, spotting something. He gasped quietly then stared at it for a few seconds. He picked it up and mumbled,

"What the heck?" then stood up straight.

"Hi, are you Mr Waterhouse?" A gentle female voice called from behind him. Trey refused to turn around. He held it in front of him making it impossible for her to see, then looked over his shoulder and said to her,

"Hey, I'm just tidying up. Go straight in she's upstairs in the far room to your right." The carer nodded then walked through the unlocked door, minding her business.

***

Trey dragged his feet one in front of the other as he entered the gym like a zombie. He walked over to the reception desk and asked the receptionist,

"Where's Kaleel?"

"He's over there training someone." The receptionist answered and pointed at Kaleel over by the weights. Trey dragged his feet over to Kaleel and the woman he is training. Spotting Trey, Kaleel politely excused himself then walked over to him.

"What's good brother?" Kaleel asked then shook his hand.

"Come to the back for a minute," Trey said with an overwhelmed look on his face. Knowing something is wrong with

Trey, Kaleel walked back over to the lady and told her to carry on lifting before he followed Trey into their office. Trey walked over to his desk, sat down then pulled it out of his pocket and dropped it onto the table.

"What's that?" Kaleel asked as he walked over to Trey's desk. Noticing Trey wasn't saying anything back, Kaleel picked up the flat and folded empty box. He unravelled it then read the packaging before he asked, "Ayisha's pregnant?" as he looked up from the home pregnancy test kit.

"I don't know." Trey managed to say as he shrugged.

"Then whose is it? Chyna's?" Kaleel guessed then sat down feeling overwhelmed too.

"I don't know. I found it in the bin." Trey told him before he sat down.

"We both know that you've slept with Chyna and Ayisha, so what if they're both pregnant?" Kaleel guessed.

"I only found one, so it could be either of theirs," Trey said dreadfully.

"Okay, but if they're both pregnant then that would be crazy. Your ex and your new girl both pregnant and living with you." Kaleel laughed then looked at Trey's worried face. He stopped laughing, then suggested, "why don't we Google some pregnancy symptoms? You've been living with them, so you should be able to see if they've shown any." Trey nodded effortlessly then watched Kaleel take his phone out and start searching. Trey waited for only a few seconds until he heard Kaleel read out loud, "from what I can see, some symptoms would be tender swollen breasts, fatigue, slight bleeding and cramping."

"Swollen breasts?" Trey repeated interrupting Kaleel.

"Yeah, why?" Kaleel asked intrigued to hear the answer.

"Because Ayisha's breasts have grown huge lately, but it's not like I'm complaining."

"So, you think it could be Ayisha that's pregnant?"

"I don't know, she could be. I don't even know what the results were, but her breasts have definitely grown. What other symptoms have they mentioned?"

Kaleel nodded then continued to read out loud,

"Nausea with or without being sick, constantly using the toilet."

"Are you serious?" Trey interrupted him again. Kaleel looked up from his phone, then watched Trey pounce up and rush over to his side of the desk before he took his phone and read the rest of the symptoms.

"What?" Kaleel asked eager to know what Trey is thinking.

Trey looked up from Kaleel's phone then told him,

"Chyna's been complaining about using the toilet more than usual and once when we went out, Ayisha had some random mood swings and felt sick when she smelt her food."

With a blank look on his face, thinking the worst Kaleel asked,

"What if they're both pregnant?"

Trey froze for a few seconds then replied,

"I don't know man! But if Chyna is pregnant then the doctors would have told me at the hospital."

Kaleel shook his head disagreeing with Trey then said,

"Not necessarily, she could have told them not to say anything."

Trey sighed heavily then handed Kaleel his phone before he said,

"I don't know man, if Ayisha's pregnant then I'm all for it, but if Chyna is… then I know Ayisha will be pissed."

Fearing the outcome, Kaleel decided to ask,

"So, what are you going to do?"

Trey shook his head then said,

"I don't know, because I can't ask Ayisha right now."

Immediately Kaleel asked,

"Why can't you?"

"I can but I'm not going to do it over the phone. She went back to LA this morning because work needed her."

"I thought they were fine with her working down here," Kaleel said.

"So, did I. I mean they're cool with it, but they needed her down there, so she had to go," Trey said feeling slightly bitter inside because he misses her.

"Aww okay, I see. You can always ask Chyna." Kaleel suggested which made Trey think.

***

Trey let himself into his house then made his way straight into the living room to see Chyna sitting on the sofa, eating a sweetcorn and tuna sandwich.

"Hey," Chyna called with her mouth full of food.

He nodded then noted that Chyna is eating sweetcorn.

"Since when did you start eating sweetcorn? You used to hate it," Trey reminded her, then watched her finish what was in her mouth and listened to her answer,

"I know right. Kimberly made me this and it tastes *soooo* good." Looking at Chyna suspiciously and dreadfully, Trey nodded then heard her add in an excited tone, "I'm glad you finally kicked Ayisha out. I guess you can say this is my victory meal." Looking at Chyna like she is crazy, he asked in a confused tone,

"What are you talking about?"

Chyna rolled her eyes then explained,

"Obviously you realised how wrong Ayisha was for attacking me yesterday and got rid of her... that's why she's not here silly."

"Oh nah, Ayisha had to fly back to LA for a few days."

Feeling enraged and disheartened, Chyna dropped her half-eaten sandwich on to the sofa, then asked,

"You're still together?"

"Of course! She's my world and she isn't going nowhere." Trey stated, then stood up and headed towards the door.

Flights:

Ayisha and her colleagues worked extremely hard as a team, which resulted in them completing the project way earlier than expected. So Ayisha booked the earliest flight possible, just so she could get home and see Trey. Even though they were only away from each other for two days, it felt much longer. They made sure they were constantly messaging each other, but it wasn't the same as being with each other. With her feet pressed on the gas harder than usual, Ayisha rushed home driving over the speed limit. She parked on their drive, retrieved her mini suitcase from the trunk, then rushed into the house. Ayisha closed the door behind her, left her suitcase by the door, then rushed into the living room and gasped at what she saw.

"Oh," Ayisha mouthed as she watched Trey shiver in shock from Ayisha's unexpected appearance. He stood there holding onto Chyna, as they both laughed joyfully with Kimberly. He is smiling because he has just witnessed Chyna take a few steps into his arms. "What's all this?" Ayisha asked in an annoyed tone.

"Hey," Trey called happy to see that Ayisha is home. He reached for Chyna's crutches, handed them to her then rushed over to Ayisha. He tried to kiss her, but she moved away and looked at Kimberly who is helping Chyna. Already feeling awkward and not wanting to make a bad first impression, Ayisha turned around and headed over to her suitcase with Trey following. "I missed you. Why didn't you tell me you were coming home?" Trey asked Ayisha. Still feeling annoyed, Ayisha ignored him then silently picked up her suitcase and headed up the stairs.

Trey followed her into their room, then watched her rest her suitcase on their bed before she began to unzip it.

"Babe, why didn't you tell me that you were coming home?" Trey repeated then continued to watch her unzip her suitcase. Realising she is upset, he asked curiously, "did I do something?" He is oblivious to why Ayisha is giving him the silent treatment. She silently rested the top of her suitcase onto the bed, then took a deep breath before she told him without making eye contact,

"I come home to see you two looking all cosy."

"We weren't cosy. Chyna just surprised me that's all."

"Well you both looked comfortable to me, I'm sure you looked cosy to the carer too," Ayisha said as she finally looked at him. Trey laughed as he realised Ayisha is being jealous.

"It wasn't like that," Trey paused then walked over to her and held onto her waist, "I promise you it was completely harmless. Look, I don't want to argue with you especially not over her." Feeling his hands on her waist and his breath on her neck made her feel weak because she missed his touch.

She sighed heavily then turned around to face him before she said,

"Okay, you're right... I didn't tell you because I wanted to surprise you."

"Well, you did," Trey told her then leaned forward to kiss her before his phone rang.

"Answer it." Ayisha insisted, then turned around and looked at her full suitcase that isn't going to unpack itself. He nodded then slid his phone out of his grey and white Puma joggers.

"Hey, Ma," Trey answered then heard Claire reply,

"Hey son, how's everything going?"

"It's going really well cause Ayisha's back."

"Aww, good cause you were missing her like crazy. I know you usually text me now and then but gosh, my thumbs were tired of typing."

Trey laughed then said,

"Yeah, I did I missed her, but how are you?"

"I'm fine. I was just checking in to see if you've gotten rid of that demon yet?"

Trey sighed then confessed,

"No, I haven't yet. But it won't be for now."

"Trey Waterhouse, you listen to me and you listen to me very closely. You're going to lose Ayisha if you keep that devil child around."

Interrupting Claire, not wanting to hear any more, he replied,

"Okay, Ma, I'm with Ayisha right now let me enjoy being with her," before he hung up.

Whilst unpacking Ayisha asked,

"How's Claire?"

"She's cool, just checking up on me."

"Oh okay," Ayisha replied with a slight squint in her eyes, because she heard the whole conversation due to his volume being so loud. The room went silent until Trey told her,

"Chyna thought I kicked you out."

Ayisha bellowed in laugher then asked,

"What made her think that?"

"Because you were gone. She thought I kicked you out for taking the ring back. She said that you attacked her."

Ayisha laughed after Chyna's accusation then answered,

"Oh, she wishes! All that girl does is play victim. She dishes it out but can't take it."

"Mm, I wanted to get you both together to talk the day after it happened, but you had to go."

Ayisha sucked her teeth then replied,

"There's no point. Things will always be the same as long as she's here." Trey listened then figured there's a deeper meaning to what she had said.

"What do you mean?"

"Nothing." Ayisha hummed then zipped her suitcase shut.

* * *

Ayisha's eyelids slowly opened to see the room is well lit, with the sun shining through the gaps in the blinds. She tossed over to see Trey is fast asleep snoring his head off. She can smell his morning breath and can see the dribble sliding out of his mouth, that is wide open and landing on the wet puddle on his pillow. Although he is a bad sleeper she loves waking up and seeing that view. She smiled then stretched her head close to his and pecked him on his cheek. Feeling her lips touch his cheek woke Trey up from his deep sleep. His eyes shot open to see Ayisha smiling at him.

"Morning, I missed waking up with you next to me," Ayisha confessed while still smiling.

"I did too," Trey said after he wiped away the dribble from his mouth.

"What does my baby want for breakfast?"

"Pancakes with something sweet like you," Trey answered with a smug look on his face.

Ayisha laughed after his joke then replied,

"You're so cheesy and okay pancakes it is then."

Ayisha took a step at a time down the stairs with her red feathered dressing gown trailing behind her. The smell of beans, toast and freshly brewed tea can be smelt from halfway down the stairs. As Ayisha walked closer to the kitchen, the sound of two female voices can be heard coming from behind the closed kitchen door. Ayisha stopped in front of the door then heard Chyna tell Kimberly,

"Everything was fine before she came back into the picture. He cherished and worshipped the ground I walked on. Anything I wanted he got it for me. He even gave me his card, so I could buy whatever I wanted but now it's all changed." Ayisha gasped, then listened carefully keen to see what Kimberly had to say back.

"It does look like she wears the pants in their relationship. I mean, I've only seen her for a few seconds, but she didn't seem like a nice person. She didn't even say hello to me," Kimberly paused then stated, "I must say she is a good looker, maybe that's why he's with her."

Chyna laughed then replied,

"She isn't all that! I'm going to ask Trey to buy me a new makeup kit then we'll see who's prettier." Ayisha rolled her eyes silently laughing after Chyna because she found her pathetic, plus hearing their conversation only confirmed that Chyna is intimidated by her.

"Yeah, do that," Kimberly said.

"I will, I'll show him what he's missing out on, then that home wrecker will be out of the picture."

Not being able to hear any more of their spiteful and biased conversation, Ayisha controlled her emotions then opened the door and walked in. She watched their faces display a shocked expression, then quickly turn into fake smiles.

"Hi, we haven't officially met have me? I'm Kimberly and you are?" Kimberly said then rushed over to Ayisha and held her hand out. Ayisha forced out a smile then shook Kimberly's hand while she introduced herself. "Nice to meet you Ayisha. I must say what a beauty you are. You're glowing without makeup. Look at how clear your skin is." Kimberly said kissing Ayisha's ass.

Chyna rolled her eyes then heard Ayisha answer,

"Thanks, that's what happens when you're dating the love of your life and eating well."

"Yes, indeed," Kimberly paused then rushed over to the warm beans on the stove, "I've made breakfast would you like something to eat?"

"Oh, no thanks." Ayisha declined then walked over to the kettle to check how much water is inside. "Kimberly, you've been very helpful, but we no longer require your services," Ayisha said unable to act fake any longer.

"Oh, Trey didn't say," Kimberly and Chyna said at the same time.

Unaware of what's happening in the kitchen, Trey announced,

"I smell beans!" as he jogged down the stairs with his hungry belly. He entered the kitchen to see three upset and angry women looking directly at him. He swallowed his spit nervously then wonders what's happening.

"Why have you sacked Kimberly?" Chyna confronted him in an annoyed tone. Confused, Trey looked away from Chyna to Kimberly who looked disheartened, then at Ayisha who is looking at him silently telling him to go along with her.

He stood there for a few seconds, then said,

"Because I did," before he shrugged then rushed out of hell's kitchen.

***

Trey entered the gym and walked over to the reception desk. Spotting Trey walking over to her, the receptionist smiled then refreshed the system ready for him to ask for an update.

"Hey, Trey," The receptionist greeted him.

"Hey beautiful, where's Kaleel?" Trey asked instead.

"Oh, okay, he's just started one of his training sessions." She answered then looked past him at Kaleel, who is training Terry.

"Thanks," Trey winked then tapped the desk.

Kaleel and Terry are standing next to the treadmill stretching. Terry's copying Kaleel's routine and listening to him explain the benefits of stretching.

"Hey." Trey greeted them then leant on the treadmill.

"Oh, hey Trey," Terry said as he stretched his chunky arms, then gasped for his breath.

"What's up, bro?" Kaleel asked Trey once he spotted the baffled facial expression on Trey's face.

"Women." Trey sighed then laughed after what he had just said. Terry too can see the baffled look on Trey's face, but as concerned as he is, he accepts that it isn't his place to ask.

"Ayisha or Chyna?" Kaleel asked needing clarity, then continued to stretch with Terry copying.

"Both." Trey answered then sat on the cushioned seat for lifting weights.

"Both?" Terry managed to ask unsure of how Trey is going to react. Trey looked at Terry blankly then eventually nodded. Seeing that Trey didn't bite Terry's head off and seeing how concerned Terry is, Kaleel decided to fill him in,

"He's living with his ex and his new girl."

"Really?" Terry asked calmly trying his best not to judge him or jump to conclusions.

"My ex was in a crash and had nowhere to stay, so I and my girl moved her in," Trey informed him summarising his situation.

"Okay and your partner is okay with that?" Terry asked.

"Yeah… well, I thought she was." Trey answered still feeling baffled. Terry and Kaleel looked at Trey intrigued to hear why Trey had just said that. Spotting their intrigued eyes, Trey told them, "Ayisha wanted me to get a carer to look after Chyna while she was gone, so I did, then I walk in to see Chyna was mad at me for firing the carer which I didn't do," Trey paused, "then I found out it was Ayisha who fired the carer, after she told me to get one," Trey said then shook his head not understanding women.

"Maybe she realised you didn't need the carer after all." Terry guessed.

"Maybe, I'm so confused man. It's driving me insane." Trey finally confessed. Seeing how stressed Trey is and feeling concerned for him, Terry decided to give Trey some words of advice.

"If it's making you unhappy then I suggest you make some changes. The last thing you want is to lose someone who means so much to you." Terry looked at Kaleel and Trey's faces, to see that they are actually tuned in and paying attention to his words, so he carried on, "I met your mother at university. She was the best-looking girl there and I just had to speak to her. I knew I was punching above my weight, but she was nice to me and we hit it off instantly. We got married shortly after then moved in together. Everything was perfect until she brought you home. I know that sounds bad but back then I was selfish, which I wish I wasn't. Because of my selfish ways, I lost the best thing that has ever happened to me."

Trey interrupted Terry and reminded him,

"You lost her because you walked out."

Terry nodded agreeingly then added,

"That's very true. I ran away and gave up on my relationship and look at how that ended up. Look at me now, it clearly worked out, didn't it? I'm an out of shape lonely old man.

I wish every day that I would've stayed and didn't run away when things got hard, but I can't change the past. Son, I don't know your whole situation, but if you really want your relationship to last speak to each other. Put your pride aside and make some changes, changes that you might not be comfortable with, but it will be worth it." Trey listened to every single word Terry had said, then realised he is right.

Trey nodded then said to Kaleel,

"I've got to get rid of Chyna." Kaleel nodded, still absorbing the advice he had just heard from Terry, then agreed,

"Yeah, you have too."

* * *

While Trey was at the gym, Ayisha and Chyna stayed home. Ayisha wasted no time in getting rid of Kimberly. She helped her to pack and sent her on her way after thanking her for her service. As Ayisha cooks – making sure Trey's food is ready for when he gets home, Chyna lay on the sofa with her legs resting on a pile of cushions watching TV. Ayisha entered the living room carrying a tray with Chyna's food on.

"Here," Ayisha called as she handed Chyna the tray. Still being annoyed with Ayisha for getting rid of Kimberly, Chyna took the tray from Ayisha then rested it on her lap refusing to say anything to her. She looked down into the plate at the creamy mashed potatoes and well-seasoned sticky BBQ ribs, which made her mouth water. Hearing Ayisha re-enter the living room, Chyna swallowed her saliva and watched Ayisha carry her tray over and sit down on the sofa. Chyna's eyes skimmed Ayisha's naturally clear skin then looked down into her plate, which looked more neatly presented than hers. Not liking that and wanting to get under Ayisha's skin, Chyna looked onto the table to see her half-empty glass of Ribena. She looked at it for a few seconds then came up with a petty idea. She reached forward with her tray on her lap, pretending to reach for her drink, which resulted in her tray surfing off her lap and her food splattering all over the floor.

"Argh," Chyna said trying her best to hold back her laughter.

"Really?" Ayisha sucked her teeth then looked at the food on the floor. She rested her tray on the space between them then said to Chyna, "you did that on purpose!"

"I didn't, I thought I could reach it. I didn't want to bother you," Chyna lied.

With an unimpressed look on her face, Ayisha replied,

"Well, you can sit in that mess," then picked up her tray and began to eat her food.

"Are you serious?" Chyna asked in disbelief.

"Very!" Ayisha replied bluntly.

"Put your damn food down and clean up my mess right now!" Chyna demanded which angered Ayisha. Unable to control herself anymore, Ayisha suddenly saw red and snapped. She dropped her tray onto the space between them, jumped up and pointed at Chyna, "you're disrespectful and spiteful; I've really had enough of you!"

"No, I'm not you are! You bloody homewrecker."

"Me? A homewrecker?" Ayisha repeated in shock.

"Yes, you! Who else is here?" Chyna asked belittling her.

"You're right no one else is here. That means Trey isn't here to protect you right now." Ayisha threatened her.

"Oh, is that right? What are you going to do to me then? Break my other leg? That wouldn't be the first time I've heard that threat."

"Maybe," Ayisha said whilst feeling her blood boil.

"Go on then I dare you, cause you'll be doing me a favour. Then Trey and I can finally get back together." Hearing those exact words triggered Ayisha even more. She marched over to Chyna, stood over her and yanked her up by her clothes.

"Let go of me!" Chyna commanded as she looked into Ayisha's enraged eyes.

"Hell no," Ayisha barked then stepped back and dragged Chyna up to her feet.

"My leg!" Chyna bellowed as she put pressure onto her foot. Ayisha refused to say anything back and couldn't because she's too angry. Ayisha dragged Chyna by her arm over to her unused wheelchair in the corner of the living room. With each step Chyna took, she felt a warm sharp pain running up and down her leg. "Let go!" Chyna panicked before she was thrown into the wheelchair. "What are you doing?" Chyna screamed as she is being wheeled quickly out of the living room. Still seeing red, Ayisha ignored her then suddenly stopped once they reached the back door. While Ayisha unlocked it, Chyna tried her best to stand up and escape, but she couldn't. Once she put pressure onto her foot the pain tripled, so she sat back down and screamed at the top of her lungs. Ayisha opened the back door then wheeled Chyna outside into the garden. She then walked over to the garden hose, picked it up and pointed it at Chyna.

"No, don't!" Chyna pleaded then watched Ayisha turn it on and felt cold water gush onto her face. Chyna sat in her wheelchair karate chopping the water as she choked, begging Ayisha to stop. After doing this for a minute, Ayisha turned off the hose then dropped it onto the grass as she told her,

"You've got a smart mouth, so it had to be washed out," before she walked into the house and locked the door behind her.

***

Trey parked onto his drive, then rushed into the house feeling determined and inspired.

"Baby," Trey called then rushed into the living room to see it is empty. Instead of finding Ayisha, he spotted a tray and food spilt on the floor. He stood there for a few seconds wondering what had happened, then decided to carry on looking for Ayisha. "Ayisha." He called as he checked the kitchen and the dining room to see they were both empty. He jogged up the stairs and checked their room, to see that is empty also. He left their room then checked his office and the two spare rooms to see they are empty. After checking the bathroom, Trey decided to check the room that Chyna is occupying. He tapped on the door gently then let himself in to see Chyna isn't home either. He stood in the middle of the doorway, mind blown, wondering where they both are. He pulled out his phone with the intention to call Ayisha until he heard the doorbell ring. Assuming it is Ayisha and Chyna at the door, Trey quickly jogged down the stairs and opened it to see Mr and Mrs Jones standing there.

They are an old Caucasian couple who have been living next door for over 25 years. Mrs Jones is a kind old lady, who tends to her front and back garden daily, but she is also a nosey human being. She is the first to know if anyone has a visitor and never shies away from any gossip. Whereas, Mr Jones is someone who doesn't like or listen to gossip. They are the perfect example of a Ying and Yang couple. All Mr Jones does is focus on his family, read his newspapers and smoke his pipes, living lavishly off his retirement fund.

"Hi Trey, we're sorry to bother you." Mr Jones said in his tired and weak voice.

"Yeah, we really are but today we noticed something rather strange." Mrs Jones added.

"It's okay, what was it?" Trey asked worrying for Ayisha's safety.

"Well, I heard some screaming and shouting earlier on, so I decided to check it out. I followed the screaming and found that it was coming from your garden. I managed to look through a gap in the fence to see Chyna was outside," Mrs Jones paused still feeling shocked. Not only was she shocked that she found Chyna outside, she was also shocked that Chyna had moved back in with Trey. She was under the impression that Chyna had moved out and was gone forever after she nearly burnt down his house. "We found Chyna outside soaking wet in a wheelchair and locked outside." Mrs Jones told him uncomfortably.

"What?" Trey said in shock not believing what he had just heard.

"Don't worry we didn't call the police." Mr Jones assured Trey before Mrs Jones added,

"We nearly did! But Mr Jones assured me there must be a reason why she was outside." Not believing what he had just heard, Trey stood there gobsmacked unable to speak.

"Son, do you want to come with us and see her?" Mr Jones offered.

"She's at our house. We had to break into your garden and get her out of those wet clothes." Mrs Jones added.

"Please," Trey nodded, then closed the door behind him and followed them in their house into the living room. Their walls have lime green wallpaper with light grey patterns on. The floor is multicoloured with an Indian rug in the centre. The curtains are dark brown which compliments the variety of plants and antiques scattered around the room. Hanging from the walls are frames with hand-painted animals. On the sand coloured sofa next to the vintage piano lay Chyna who is fast asleep. Trey looked around the room hoping to see Ayisha, but she isn't there.

"Was it just Chyna outside or was there another woman with her?" Trey asked.

"Oh, no love. I saw Ayisha carrying a few suitcases into her car before she sped off." Mrs Jones gossiped.

"Trey?" Chyna called as she forced herself to sit up.

"Hey," Trey said with his mind elsewhere worrying about Ayisha.

"That bitch threw me outside and turned the hose on me," Chyna complained dramatically entertaining Mrs Jones. Not wanting the neighbours, especially Mrs Jones to know about their business, Trey rushed over to Chyna and helped her up to her feet while telling her,

"We'll talk about it when we get home."

"Don't forget her wheelchair." Mr Jones reminded him, then rushed off and wheeled it into the living room.

"Thank you," Trey said then helped Chyna sit in it. Once she was secured into the wheelchair, Trey said to Mr and Mrs Jones, "thanks for looking after her," then wheeled her towards the front door.

"WAIT, I had to change her." Mrs Jones called, as she picked up a plastic bag with Chyna's drenched clothes inside and handed it to him.

"Oh, thanks, I'll drop your gown back over later," Trey said then took the bag off her and rushed home.

Without closing the door properly, Trey wasted no time in questioning Chyna,

"Where's Ayisha? And what happened?"

"That crazy bitch locked me in the garden and turned the hose on me," Chyna spoke quickly without stumbling on her words.

"But why?" Trey quizzed her still confused as to why Ayisha would randomly do that. "You must have said something to upset her." Chyna screwed up her face, hating the fact that he knew Ayisha so well.

"No, I didn't, she randomly switched on me." Chyna lied then turned around to face him and made the face he once loved seeing. He looked at her face then wheeled her into the living room and helped her to get out. "We should call the police," Chyna suggested as she played the victim role.

"We could but I'm sure they'd want to know the whole situation and why all of this started," Trey answered hinting that they'd need to know what Chyna had done too.

"Oh, maybe not then," Chyna answered quickly, then looked at the food that was spilt onto the floor.

"What happened there?" Trey asked as he held her up while inspecting the food with his eyes.

Chyna ignored his question then said,

"Just sit me there," then pointed at the seat Ayisha would always sit on.

"Okay." Trey nodded then lowered her onto the seat and handed her the remote. "Here, I'm just going to call Ayisha."

***

The front door opened and there stood the Clarke's maid in her black and white uniform holding onto a duster in her hand. With her head bowed, Ayisha heard the maid greet her,

"Hi, Ayisha, how are you?"

"I'm fine thanks," Ayisha answered then entered her parent's house with her head still bowed. "Where's my mother?" Ayisha mumbled.

"She's in the second living room."

"Mom," Ayisha called as she entered the living room to see the back of Tanya, who is sitting on the cream sofa with gold plated legs shopping for a new chandelier.

"Baby girl," Tanya called cheerfully then turned around to see Ayisha's puffy eyes. "Ayisha," Tanya called as she stood up. She started to walk over to Tanya then ran into her open arms. Feeling her mother's embrace made her feel safe, which made her burst into tears. "Oh, Ayisha," Tanya said while rubbing her back, "let it all out baby girl it's okay to cry." They stood there hugging for a few minutes until Ayisha wiped away her tears then sat down on the sofa. "What's the matter?" Tanya asked in her calm but worried voice.

"It's Trey." Ayisha said then cried into her hands. Tanya picked up the box of tissues from the table, carried them over to Ayisha then handed them to her before she sat down.

"What about him? Did he cheat on you?" Tanya guessed then watched Ayisha shake her head, disagreeing with her.

"Then what is it?" Tanya asked.

Ayisha dried her face, took a deep breath before she answered,

"I've lost him."

"Lost him how?" Tanya asked confused, trying to make sense of it all.

"I did something stupid," Ayisha wheezed, "I wasn't thinking I just did it and now I've driven them into each other's arms," Ayisha said then started to cry again.

"No, you haven't because I know for a fact Trey isn't that stupid... Tell me what did you do?" Tanya asked as she continued to rub Ayisha's back comforting her.

"I'm so stupid," Ayisha said repeatedly until Tanya stopped her,

"Ayisha stop that! I'm going to make us some tea and when I come back you should have calmed down." Tanya said then walked off.

Tanya re-entered the living room a few minutes after, carrying two cups of teas over to Ayisha. She watched Ayisha decline Trey's call then stood up to get two mats for their teas to rest on.

"Are you okay now?" Tanya asked as she rested them onto the mats.

"Yeah, I am." Ayisha nodded then watched Tanya sit down next to her.

"Good, now tell me what happened."

"Mom you were right all along. I was so stupid to ever think that it was okay to move his ex in with us. All Chyna's done since she moved in is taunt me and do my head in," Ayisha paused, "she pushed me to my limits and I snapped."

Fearing what Ayisha is about to tell her, Tanya asked,

"What did you do?"

"She kept trying me and running her smart mouth, so I put her outside and turned the hose on her."

Tanya sighed in relief then laughed,

"You put the hose on her?"

"I know, I shouldn't have done that, but she was getting to me. She even told me to hit her so Trey could see and then they'd finally get back together."

"It sounds like she deserved what she got," Tanya said trying to make Ayisha feel better.

Ayisha sighed then shook her head.

"Mom, I don't feel the same anymore. I was kidding myself when I agreed to let her stay with us. I only did it to make Trey happy, but instead it's made me miserable. I've lost myself."

"Lost yourself how?" Tanya asked not understanding what she meant.

Ayisha's phone began to ring. She looked at it to see it's Trey calling, so she declined it.

"This whole situation was too much for me to handle. I've never been around someone so bitter with such a dark heart. She was always saying something smart and throwing digs at me. Mom at one point I imagined poisoning her." Ayisha confessed then heard Tanya gasp.

"Exactly, being around her has drained me and I feel like I've changed. I don't know who I am anymore. Maybe being with Trey isn't worth it after all."

Tanya gasped then reminded her,

"You love Trey. You two were meant to be together... do you remember how excited you were when he messaged you?"

Ayisha nodded then replied in a fed-up tone,

"I know, but it isn't worth me losing who I truly am for him. Clearly, she wants him that bad, so she can just have him."

"That's ridiculous! He loves you and you love him. You were reunited for a reason and I believe that. You can't give up now when things get hard."

"Mom, I must. I'm not the same person anymore. I've done things that I would never have imagined doing." Ayisha said feeling disappointed in herself.

"And that's okay, we all get angry at times. We're all human."

"I know, but I can't do this anymore. I've already booked a flight to go back to LA."

"But you've not long come back. Don't go Ayisha. Stay and we'll sort this out," Tanya pleaded.

"No, mom, it's okay. I need some time to myself. I need to find myself again and remember who I am."

"Ayisha, me and your father will help you. We'll get you the best therapist that money can buy, we'll do anything, please don't go."

"It's okay there's no need too. This is something that I need to do by myself." Tanya sighed finally understanding that Ayisha had made up her mind and accepted the fact she wasn't going to change it.

"I don't want you to go... but I understand that you feel this is something you need to do," Tanya paused then offered, "if you want, I'm more than happy to come with you."

"Thank you but it's okay. I really need to do this by myself." Ayisha said meaning every single word.

Tanya sighed then offered,

"Okay, why don't you leave your car here. That way you'll know that it's safe. I'll drop you to the airport." Ayisha considered her offer, agreed then hugged her tightly.

* * *

Leroy sat at the head of the table in the meeting room listening to all the fresh ideas that are being thrown around, suggesting innovating ways for his empire to keep growing. Usually, if anyone wanted to get in contact with Leroy, then they would call his office and his receptionist would schedule them in, but if his personal phone rang then he knew that the call was important. One of Leroy's employees stood in front of the projector suggesting a few of his ideas until they all heard Leroy's personal phone start to ring. Leroy got up then politely excused himself from their meeting. He closed the glass door behind him then answered the call,

"Tanya?" he called wondering what the emergency is.

"Ayisha's gone back to LA! I've just dropped her off at the airport." Tanya informed him in an upset tone.

"What? Why did she leave so suddenly? Why didn't she say goodbye?"

"She said that she called the office, but you were in a meeting, so she will call you when she lands. The reason why she left is because of Trey! That man needs a good talking to."

"What did he do?"

"He broke our little girls' heart. I mean he didn't cheat on her, but his actions have hurt her. Who in their right mind lets their ex move back in with them? Especially Chyna?"

"What?" Leroy asked in a confused tone, "when did this happen?"

"Nearly a month now. I didn't say anything because I wanted Ayisha to tell you herself. It happened the same day they paid Chyna off. She got into a car accident and they ended up taking her back in," Tanya told him.

"But why would she even agree to that nonsense?" Leroy asked feeling disappointed.

"She fooled herself into thinking that it was a good idea. I did warn her, but she refused to listen and did it for Trey."

Leroy sighed then said,

"Okay, I'll call you later."

"Are you going to talk to him?" Tanya guessed needing clarity.

"Yes, right now," Leroy told her then politely ended their call and called Trey.

"Hello?" Trey answered unsure of what to expect.

"I've just received a call from my wife telling me that our daughter has flown back to LA because of you," Leroy answered getting straight to the point, showing how angry he is.

In shock, Trey repeated,

"She's gone back to LA?"

"Yes, because of you! I'm so angry that I can't go back to my meeting. We need to talk right now."

"I'm sorry," Trey apologised then suggested, "I can come to your gym if you're still in Houston."

"No, don't bother I'll come to yours instead."

***

Leroy entered Trey's gym and headed straight over to the reception desk.

"Welcome, how may I assist you today?" The receptionist asked then spotted Leroy's annoyed facial expression.

"I'm here to see my son in law, Trey," Leroy answered then heard her say,

"Oh okay, unfortunately, Trey isn't here." She watched Leroy's blank face, then said, "I'll just give him a call," before she picked up the phone and rang Trey. Leroy took a few steps away from the desk and scanned the gym with his eyes liking what he is seeing. He is impressed by the high-end equipment and how occupied the gym is. "Excuse me sir, unfortunately, he isn't answering." The receptionist told him before Trey entered the gym.

"I got here as fast as I could," Trey told Leroy. He turned around to face Trey to see his face is pale, and his eyes are full of red veins.

"Let's speak in your office," Leroy suggested feeling bad for Trey. He nodded then led the way into his and Kaleel's office. Leroy followed Trey into the office then headed over to his desk. Trey automatically walked over to his seat, then remembered who he is talking to, so he walked over to the opposite seat, and out of respect offered Leroy his. "I was furious before I got here but seeing your face shows me that you care about what's going on," Leroy said as he sat in Trey's chair.

"I do," Trey assured him.

"I'm glad you do. I know you don't have any children yet, so you can't relate to how I'm feeling but I am very pissed. I got a call from my wife who is very upset, telling me that our baby girl's hurting so badly that she can't stay home. This angers me deeply." Leroy said firmly.

Trey nodded as he listened to Leroy say,

"Today I was told that you and Ayisha have been living with Chyna... Who in their right mind does that? What type of sick fantasy world are you living in?"

Trey interrupted him and tried to defend himself,

"It isn't a sick fantasy world, Chyna needed somewhere to stay so we took her in. I asked Ayisha first just to see what she thought and she was fine with it."

Leroy looked at Trey sideways then asked,

"You really believed Ayisha was okay with having your ex-fiancée, the woman that you planned on spending the rest of your life with, move back in with you," Leroy paused then thought of something, "have you ever been to counselling or spoken to someone?" Trey glanced at Leroy wondering why he'd ask such a random question. Not wanting to disrespect Leroy, Trey asked,

"No, what would make you ask such a question?"

Wasting no time, Leroy immediately answered,

"I would advise you to do because I think it would help."

"No disrespect but help me with what?" Trey asked puzzled.

Leroy cleared his throat then explained,

"I believe you're still hurting from what you went through as a child, with your mother." Hearing this brought emotions that Trey hasn't felt in over a decade. Leroy watched Trey slouch and bow his head then continued, "my wife and I were aware of how badly your mother was treating you and we even spoke to her, but she refused to listen. So, on the day that we left, we called social services and look how well that worked out." Trey looked up at Leroy feeling completely shocked. This was news to him. He had no idea they were aware of what went on inside his home and that they even took the time to speak to her. It also made him realise that he is secretly hurting. Trey could feel his eyes begin to fill up with tears, so he clutched his fist then rested his back against the chair trying his best to hold them back. "Son, I know you're hurting. I think that's why you keep Chyna around," Leroy said then stood up and walked over to him, "let it out." Leroy said then watched Trey continue to fight back his tears. "You need to forgive, let go and move on. Let happiness in because you deserve it." Unable to fight the tears anymore, Trey lost his battle and felt a gush of tears explode out of his eyes. He leant forward and rested his forehead into his hands then felt the tears slide off his face and onto his lap. "That's right let it out," Leroy said then tapped Trey's back a few times. Trey wiped away his tears then looked behind him at Leroy's concerned eyes.

"I really didn't mean to hurt Ayisha," Trey confessed sincerely, as he worked hard on stopping himself from crying.

"I know," Leroy nodded then walked back over to his seat and sat down. "You have someone special in your life. Someone who's beautiful and has a heart of gold. Ayisha's a rare gem. She really cares about you, she always has. You've been battling demons you weren't even aware of. My advice to you is that you get some counselling and get rid of Chyna, she's toxic and dangerous."

"I will," Trey nodded then used his hands to wipe his face again.

"Good, you've got Claire by your side, as well as me and my wife too. You're going to get through this." Leroy watched Trey stand up, so he did the same, then watched him raise his hand ready for them to shake hands.

"Thank you. I really appreciate it and I'm sorry once again."

***

Trey slowly walked into his house and closed the door behind him to hear Chyna on the phone.

"Trey?" She called then ended the call. He heard her call for him but ignored her and walked into the living room like a zombie. Seeing Chyna sitting in Ayisha's space, reminded him that he had to clean up the food that is on the floor. "Where were you?" Chyna questioned him then watched him walk around the sofa and head into the kitchen. "Trey." She called again but heard no reply.

He re-entered the living room with the dustpan and brush in his hand, then knelt on the floor and started to sweep up the mashed potato and BBQ ribs.

"Ayisha whacked my food out of my hand." Chyna lied playing the victim role again.

"Mm," Trey said as he continued to clean up.

"Seriously Trey, she just wanted to fight me for some reason. She even said she wanted to break my other leg." Hearing Chyna's voice and what he believed to be as lies agitated him. He looked up at Chyna then told her clearly,

"I want you out by the end of the week."

Chyna gasped as she rested her hands on her chest,

"Why? Where am I supposed to go?"

"I don't know," Trey shrugged, "call whoever you were on the phone too."

"But why?" Chyna whined.

"I just need you out of here. You can walk now so you'll be fine."

"I can hardly walk!" Chyna stated as she watched him helplessly.

"I'm giving you until the end of this week. That's more than enough time to sort your living arrangements out." Trey said then left everything on the floor and walked off.

***

Trey left his en-suite bathroom and walked over to the window in his boxers to close the curtains. He looked down at the empty space on the drive next to his car, then sighed because he's missing Ayisha. He closed the curtains then turned off the light and climbed into bed. He moved across to lay on Ayisha's side of the bed, then sniffed the covers and smile for what lasted two seconds. He moved along the bed, then reached for his phone and sent a text message to Ayisha,

I know you're not talking to me
but I miss and love you so much! I've
told Chyna that she's got to be out by the
end of the week. I also spoke with your dad
and he advised me to get some counselling,
so I will try first thing in the morning.

***

Trey parked outside of the house then got out and made his way to the front door. He knocked twice, then waited patiently to be let in.

"Hi, son," Claire said then hugged him.

"Hey Ma, how are you?" Trey asked then followed her into the kitchen.

"I'm okay, I've just finished making some fried chicken and white rice," Claire said as she stirred her home-made gravy.

Inhaling the combination of aromas made Trey excited. He waited for Claire to move away from the stove before he rushed over, opened the oven and grabbed a crispy coated chicken leg.

"Hey!" Claire laughed then tapped his hand playfully. He joined in the laughter then took a big bite forgetting it is hot. He pulled the chicken out of his mouth and gasped for air, hoping that it would cool his burning tongue. "That's what you get!" Claire teased as she took two plates out, ready to dish out their food.

"Thanks Ma," Trey said before he blew on his chicken leg trying to cool it down. Although Ayisha had only been gone for a full day, he misses her cooking and can't wait to eat a home-cooked meal.

"No problem, how are you?" Claire asked as she placed the first scoop of rice onto the plate.

"I'm good; I've just come back from a counselling session."

Claire stopped what she was doing, turned around and asked,

"For what?" Trey finished what was in his mouth then filled Claire in with everything that was going on in his life,

"Chyna and Ayisha must have had a fight, then Ayisha left me and Leroy spoke to me and advised me to get some counselling."

"Wow," Claire said, "I never knew you were going through so much. It's a shame about Ayisha, it sounds like she just needs time to herself. But why did you get counselling?"

"Leroy made me realise I still have issues from my upbringing. The therapist basically said that I allow Chyna to get away with so much because of that. It was actually quite insightful and I'm really glad I went." Claire nodded proudly then continued to make his plate. "Guess what?" Trey teased Claire.

"What?" Claire asked unsure of what to guess.

"I've told Chyna that she needs to be out by the end of the week."

"Thank you Jesus!" Claire said out loud then looked up to the ceiling gratefully. Claire handed Trey his plate then heard him thank her, just before his phone started to ring. He took out his phone and noticed that it is Ayisha calling. "Hey," He answered then listened extra hard for her response.

"Hey… I read your text." Ayisha said quietly.

"Good, how are you?" Trey asked desperate to hear the answer.

"I'm okay… you said you spoke to my dad." Ayisha reminded him wanting to know more. He looked at Claire's tuned in eyes then smiled confirming that it is Ayisha.

"Yeah, I did. He told me that I should get some counselling which I did, I went today."

"Oh really? That's good how was it?" Ayisha asked curiously.

"Pretty good," Trey answered then reminded her, "I've told Chyna that she's got to be out by the end of the week… Will you be coming home anytime soon? Cause I miss you."

Ayisha took a few seconds to reply then told him,

"I can come home today *but only* on one condition."

"Anything, just tell me what to do and I'll do it," Trey begged excitedly.

"I want Chyna gone today!"

"Today?" Trey repeated in shock. The silence on the line told Trey that Ayisha is very serious. "Okay, anything for you," Trey said quickly.

"Good, I'll book a flight for later today then I'll call you once I've landed for you to pick me up," Ayisha told him calmly.

"Okay, I'll see you later, love you," Trey said happily before she ended the call. "I've got to go," Trey said as he headed towards the door carrying his plate of food.

"Where are you going with my plate?" Claire called then heard him shout,

"I'll bring it back later."

* * *

Trey entered the house carrying the empty plate in his hand. He drove home as fast as he could, while eating, with only one goal on his mind.

"Had enough time to think this over?" Chyna asked as she spotted him enter the living room with a massive smile on his face.

"Yeah, I did," Trey said as he walked past her and headed towards the kitchen.

"Really?" Chyna said with a heart full of hope.

"Yeah, I need you out today." She gasped loudly in her seat then looked behind her, just in time to see that he had just entered the kitchen.

"What? Where am I supposed to go? You said the end of the week." Chyna reminded him as she looked directly at the kitchen door, then saw him poke his head through to look at her and say,

"I know, but I've changed my mind."

"But, but, but where am I meant to go? Tyanna can't take me in." Chyna said.

"You'll figure it out," Trey said and poured himself some orange juice to wash down the food he had just eaten.

"Treyyy," Chyna whined then watched him re-enter the living room.

"I'm just going to pack your stuff," Trey announced as he walked past her without making any eye contact.

He carelessly yanked Chyna's clothes off the hangers and threw them into her suitcase. He reminisced on the time he tried to kick her out before but didn't get to because of her coughing fit. This only reassured him of how much Chyna's health has improved. Once he finished packing all her stuff, he carried both of her suitcases down the stairs where Chyna is standing with her crutches.

"You're actually serious," Chyna stated in a disheartened tone as she hopped out of the way for Trey to get past.

"Yep, did you get around to calling anyone?" Trey asked as he placed the suitcases onto the floor next to the front door.

"No, I didn't," Chyna confessed then watched him fetch her phone and hand it to her.

"Try now or else you'll be homeless, and I don't want that to happen," Trey said. She looked down at her phone in his hand, then reached for it whilst trying to balance. She grabbed it off him then rang 'Jack'. Trey leaned against the wall then crossed his arms as he watched her. Feeling him watching her, Chyna rolled her eyes then listened for an answer.

"Hey, Jack. I'm sorry to ask but I need a place to stay... like right now." Chyna told him awkwardly. She nodded a few times listening to what Jack had to say, then replied,

"Okay, thank you! I'll text you the address," before she ended their call.

"Looks like you had somewhere to stay all along," Trey said then watched her punch the address in and send it to Jack. Chyna ignored him, placed her phone into her bra then used her crutches to assist herself into the living room. He can see how upset she is becoming, which made him realise he doesn't want her to leave with them being on bad terms. He followed Chyna into the living room and watched her rest her crutches onto the arm of the sofa, then sit in Ayisha's seat silently. "Look I don't want you to be mad at me." Trey said breaking the silence, "you needed somewhere to stay so we took you in. We both knew this wasn't going to be permanent."

"I wish it was," Chyna blurted out suddenly, "I wish every day you didn't search for Ayisha. I wish every day she didn't come back into the picture. I wish every day you got over her years ago! You had me questioning if I was ever enough." Trey listened to her pour her heart out finally understanding exactly where she is coming from and why she was always acting up.

"You were enough... but I couldn't help myself. It was something that I battled with for years. You have to understand, Ayisha was the girl I planned on spending my whole life with, she was the one I pictured being there when I opened the gym and the one I planned on marrying." Trey confessed then heard Chyna sigh heavily,

"But why would you drag me along and get my hopes up, if your heart was with someone else the whole time?" Chyna asked before Trey spotted her eyes fill up with tears.

"Don't cry Chyna," Trey begged then walked over to comfort her, but she pushed him away.

"Don't touch me! Don't act like you care Trey! Just answer the question," Chyna demanded. He stumbled back then sighed regretting his actions and feeling bad for upsetting her.

"Of course I care! If I didn't care about you then I wouldn't have taken you back in after all that you've done. Look, I understand you're hurting, I really do, and I wish I didn't hurt you. But we can't take it back so the best thing for us to do is to learn from this and move on." Trey said as he looked through the window at a black Jeep that had caught his attention. He walked over to the window to see that the Jeep had pulled up and parked right behind Trey's car, blocking him in.

"Is that your friend?" Trey asked then described the car.

Chyna wiped her eyes, then cleared her throat before she asked,

"What does he look like?" Trey looked through the Jeep's window and spotted a tanned male.

Stating what he is seeing, Trey described,

"It looks like a Caucasian man," before Chyna's phone received a text.

"Yep, that's him. He's just sent me a text saying that he's outside." Chyna told him after she read the text. Wondering how Chyna knew him, but then remembering it is none of his business, Trey turned around to watch Chyna reaching for her crutches. Wanting to help her, he rushed over and helped her to get up.

"Are we good?" Trey asked once she was standing correctly.

"I guess." Chyna agreed then looked into his eyes.

"That's good," Trey said then walked back over to the window. He watched the door to the Jeep open then watched 'Jack' get out confidently. He closed the door, then turned around which gave Trey a better look at him. Seeing his face resulted in Trey's stomach suddenly dropping to the floor. He's unsure of where he has seen Jack from but is sure they've crossed paths before. From how Trey is feeling, assured him that it wasn't a good encounter.

Jack is a tall tanned male who has a premature brown beard that is starting to grow. He is also the exact build as Trey, having the muscles and height to match. His hair is combed and sprayed into a neat quiff to the side and has a silver stud in his right ear.

Watching Jack make his way over to the front door, Trey stepped back then left the living room to let him in. He opened the door to see a smug look on Jack's face, which made him remember where he knew him from.

"How the fuck do you know where I live?" Trey interrogated him as his hands folded into fists. He feels his veins suddenly pop out as his heart rate sped up.

"Aha, I hope you aren't selling drugs at your gym, or else we'll have no choice but shut it down again." It's Jack, the police officer that found the planted drugs and closed the gym.

"You really think you're the man, don't you? You're lucky you're a fed or else I'd knock your head off your shoulders," Trey threatened him.

"Stop it!" Chyna ordered feeling emotionally drained and defeated.

"You knew the officers?" Trey stated making sense of it all. Chyna did, in fact, know the officers personally. Because she knew them, it made it easier for her to get the drugs and frame Trey successfully. Once the drugs were planted, she was able to call Jack on his personal phone and give him a heads up as to where she planted them.

She had met Jack a few years back, but they became reacquainted once Chyna and Trey's relationship started to crumble. He is the one that Chyna confided in and because of this, Jack's hatred grew towards Trey. He hates how badly Chyna was treated and dislikes him because of how successful he is. Just like every other guy in Houston, he found Chyna very attractive and had been patiently waiting for the day he could scoop her up.

"Threatening an officer is a serious crime," Jack warned him with a smug look on his face, then stepped into Trey's house and reached for Chyna's suitcases.

"You don't have the right to enter my property, my private property," Trey boasted which annoyed Jack.

Freezing but looking directly at Trey, Jack said,

"Well, I guess I'll have to get another search warrant," then paused and looked around the room with his eyes, looking at all the high-end furniture that Chyna had decorated the house with. He then looked up at the crystal chandelier that hangs in the centre of the entrance, before he said, "who knows what other drugs you had to sell to afford a place like this."

"Stop it Jack!" Chyna barked then used her crutches to hop over to him, "just wait in the car," Chyna pleaded quietly. Jack looked away from Chyna then back at Trey who is standing firmly ready to fight at any moment. "Please," Chyna begged then watched him take a step back out of the house.

"I'll wait in the car for you," Jack said then took one last look at Trey before he started to walk off.

"That's right listen to your bitch," Trey shouted after him.

Chyna turned around to look at Trey then said to him sincerely,

"I'm really sorry for everything, especially for bringing him here," before she hopped forward and pecked him on his cheek. He stood there speechless unsure whether he should push her over or accept her apology. "Please carry my suitcases over to the car," Chyna asked calmly then watched him stand there disobediently. "Please, Trey," she begged then started to hop out the house towards Jack. Trey sighed then picked up her suitcases and carried them over to Jack who is leaning against the Jeep.

"Light work," Trey boasted as he carried them effortlessly like they were empty.

"Only because of all the steroids you've been taking," Jack taunted.

"I've never taken steroids and I never will. As you can see hard work pays off." Trey stated then placed the suitcases onto the floor with a smug look on his face. He looked behind him at his house and admired it, knowing that Jack is watching. Jack sucked his teeth, picked up Chyna's suitcases and threw them into the trunk, taking his anger out on them instead. "Now get the fuck off my property!" Trey demanded before he walked back into his house refusing to look back.

***

The sound of Trey's phone ringing woke him up from his nap on the sofa. He was in such a deep sleep that he isn't aware of where he is. He sat up quickly then used his hands to wipe the dribble away from his mouth. He wiped his hands on his trousers then rubbed his eyes, waking himself up. He looked through his heavy eyelids and spotted his phone spinning as it vibrated and rang on the table.

Not looking at the caller ID, he answered,

"Yo?"

"Hey, I've just landed can you come and get me?"

"Yeah, of course, just give me a sec," Trey said then hung up. Not wanting to have her waiting on him for too long, Trey got up and jogged up the stairs to wash the dribble off his face and brush his teeth.

***

Trey drove through the airport's car park holding onto his parking ticket whilst looking for Ayisha. Not seeing her, he drove closer to the airport entrance until he spotted her standing next to her suitcases. She's wearing a long red coat with black thigh boots that cover her denim jeans and a black turtleneck top to match. Spotting Ayisha's new hairstyle resulted in Trey nearly hitting a parked car, so he swerved quickly then parked next to Ayisha. After putting on his hazard lights, Trey got out of the car to hear Ayisha ask,

"Oh my gosh, are you okay?" referring to him nearly hitting the car in front.

"Yeah, I'm fine. You look amazing." Trey answered then hugged her.

"Thank you." Ayisha said then stepped out of his hug and watched him open the passenger door for her.

***

Trey drove along Burger King's drive-through, then parked behind the car ahead. Once he put on the hand brake to secure the car, Trey looked over at Ayisha and told her,

"I really like your hair," while he admired it.

"Thank you, I thought it was time for a change," Ayisha said then looked at her hair in the mirror. She looked at her black finger waves then admired her perfectly curled baby hairs.

"I love it!" Trey said still with his eyes glued to her hair looking at her like a snack.

"I'm glad you like it. I walked past a salon and thought why not?" Ayisha smiled then wasted no time in getting straight to the point, "where's Chyna?"

"She's gone." Trey paused then held onto the steering wheel and started to tap his fingers off it. Sensing something is on his mind, Ayisha asked while watching him tap his fingers,

"What happened?"

"I told her that she had to be out today which she wasn't happy about," before Ayisha interrupted him and said,

"Obviously."

He sniggered then carried on,

"She called someone to come pick her up. While we waited, we spoke about everything. I think she's got the closure she needed. But what pissed me off was the person who came to pick her up, it happened to be the same police officer that shut down the gym."

"That sneaky bitch!" Ayisha shouted then stopped herself from getting all worked up, "you know what, as long as she's out of our lives for good then I'm fine."

"That's right." Trey agreed like he was agreeing with a pastor.

After ordering and paying for their food, Trey watched the employee prepare their order. He took the bag off the employee and handed it over to Ayisha who opened the bag and made sure their order was correct before they drove off.

"Excuse me!" said Ayisha as she screwed her face. "These burgers are small as hell. I've been travelling all day and I know for a fact this won't fill me up. Can I order another burger?"

"We're not allowed to take orders at this kiosk, I'm only here to hand the food over. I can't take orders," The employee said awkwardly.

Ayisha sucked her teeth then said,

"Listen, I'm hungry so please do me this favour," then paused and took her purse out of her bag, "get me another burger and I'll give you a $20 tip." Trey looked at Ayisha then laughed not believing how rude she is acting.

"Um… okay." The employee shrugged and went to the back to get her another burger.

As Trey parked his car in the car park, for them to eat in the car, Trey said to Ayisha,

"I can't believe how rude you were to that poor kid. It isn't his fault they make the burgers small."

Ayisha laughed then waited for him to park before she said,

"It's because I'm eating for two." Trey choked on nothing as he registered what he had just heard.

"Are you serious?" He asked.

"Yep," Ayisha said with a smug look on her face.

"You're pregnant," Trey said then took his seatbelt off and squeezed her.

"Careful." Ayisha laughed then gently pushed him off her.

"Sorry, who else knows?" Trey questioned her whilst staring at her in shock.

"No one else. I wanted to tell you first." Ayisha confessed then opened her coat. She lifted her top then said, "Look," before he felt her stomach. She watched his blank but excited facial expression then told him, "I know right, I reacted the same way." He nodded without removing his eyes from her stomach then asked her,

"When did you find out?"

"I felt ill once I got to LA so I googled my symptoms and it suggested that I could be pregnant, so I took a test and it came out positive. I didn't believe it at first, so I took 4 more." Trey nodded then smiled adding everything together. He knew Ayisha had been acting different lately and expected for her to be gone for more than a day.

"It makes sense because you've been eating more than usual, plus look at those babies," Trey said referring to Ayisha's breasts. "Oh yeah, and that time at the restaurant when you felt randomly sick and emotional."

Ayisha laughed,

"I know right, it definitely makes sense!" She then grabbed Trey's hand and told him, "I want us to forget about everything that has happened and focus on us, and our family. I can actually say that I'm looking forward to the future." Still, with a big cheesy grin on his face, Trey said,

"So am I. You came back with a new hairstyle and some good news, what else?"

New beginnings:

Trey gently pressed on the brake and felt his car slow down until it stopped right outside of Kaleel's apartment block. He got out and made his way to the block of stairs. He floated up them effortlessly, because he is still on cloud 9. Once at the top, Trey stood in front of the door and knocked it impatiently. Eventually, the door swung open and there stood Kaleel in his boxers. He has red lipstick all over his face, chest and neck.

"What's up?" Kaleel asked.

"Argh, my bad." Trey apologised realising what Kaleel is up to and feeling bad for interrupting. Unable to hold it in anymore, Trey said out loud, "Ayisha's pregnant!"

"Seriously?" Kaleel asked as he registered what he had just heard in his head.

"Yeah! She came back today and told me." Still smiling in shock, Kaleel stood to the side of the door then invited Trey in, but he refused. "Are you sure?" Trey asked sceptically, "I know you're in the middle of something." Kaleel laughed and insisted for Trey to come in, before making his way towards the living room. Kaleel opened the door, then switched on the light to see the living room light up shortly after. "Are you sure she isn't going to mind?" Trey asked again.

Kaleel sucked his teeth then insisted,

"Don't worry man she'll be fine." Finally accepting that his right-hand man would rather chill with him then with some random chick, Trey nodded and threw himself onto the sofa.

"Who is she?" Trey asked curiously. Kaleel smirked proudly, refusing to tell him. Seeing Kaleel's face only increased Trey's curiosity, so he asked him a few more times until Kaleel gave in.

"Cardi."

"Cardi?" Trey mimicked him in shock, "Cardi the one that works for us on the desk?" Trey asked then watched Kaleel smile. He then pounced up like a jack in the box and pushed Kaleel playfully. "How is she?" Trey asked.

Kaleel delayed his response then reminded him,

"I don't know, you interrupted us." Trey sucked his teeth then sat down next to Kaleel before he apologised again. "It's cool... We've been kicking it for a week now." Kaleel boasted then began to laugh with Trey. Their laughs are in sync as they tap each other celebrating their good news. "But seriously congrats." Kaleel said in awe.

"Thanks." Trey said as his laugh suddenly faded.

"Do you know how far she is?"

"11 weeks." Trey answered in a proud but fearful tone.

"11 weeks? Isn't it usually months?" Kaleel asked feeling puzzled. "Yeah, that's what I said! They said she's nearly 3 months." Kaleel smiled then carried on listening to Trey. "You should see her stomach! It's so small but you can see that there's something in there," Trey paused then gazed at the wallpaper, "to think there's something actually in there... a baby... something so small that comes with such huge responsibilities." Trey said as he felt sweat forming on his forehead. Seeing Trey getting all worked up and hearing the doubt and fear in his voice, Kaleel decided to give him some words of encouragement. He held Trey's shoulder and said,

"You're going to have a son or daughter. You've finally got what you've been asking for and I'm so happy for you brother... you've got this! You've got me and your family around you, and you can't forget you've got the girl of your dreams. It's going to be something different but as I said before you've got this!" Trey listened to Kaleel's words of encouragement and appreciated them, but he can't help but worry.

"I'm going to be a dad," Trey said slowly without moving his lips properly, "what the fuck is a dad? How am I supposed to be one when I don't know what the fuck one is?" Kaleel bowed his head as he sighed, feeling Trey's pain. Just like Trey, Kaleel grew up with an absent father figure in his life. He grew up having to learn and teach himself how to be a man, but through all the trials and tribulations they both made it.

"I don't know," Kaleel confessed then added, "but you've got this, you'll figure it out. We grew up without a dad but look at us now. Two successful handsome black men who own one of Houston's biggest gyms." Trey smiled as he listened and remembered how far they have come and how well they have done, but he is still concerned.

"I don't know man," Trey said then sighed again. "I'm scared, what if I fail him... or her? What if I just up and leave?"

"Stop thinking like that! You're not Terry, you know better than to leave your family. You've got your life together. It sounds like you're forgetting you've always wanted this baby." Kaleel reminded him. "You're just scared right now and it's normal to be, if I was in your shoes I know I would be scared too. But you need to get it together cause you need to be there for Ayisha." Trey nodded then started to think of Ayisha. He pictured them being 8 years old again and replayed the conversations they used to have, of starting a family and growing old together, then he smiled. Not only is he smiling because of the conversations he had with Ayisha, but he's also smiling because he remembered Leroy. The one and only reliant and positive father figure that he's got in his life. As scared as he is, he felt a small amount of relief knowing that Leroy is still in his life. Although he isn't quite sure of how this is all going to play out, he feels better knowing that Leroy is going to be in his child's life. Then he thought of Claire, the woman with such a big heart that she took him in and raised him as her own. Then he thought of Tanya, another woman with such a big kind and caring heart. Then he thought of Kaleel and all the traits he can teach his child such as loyalty, determination and courage. Then he thought of Ayisha, he thought of her beauty, brains and patience. Then he even thought of Terry and remembered all the wise words and life experiences he has to pass down onto the next generation. Then it hit him. He is surrounded by good people with good hearts. He now knows with all his loved ones in his life, his son or daughter will grow up and become the best person they can be because of them.

"Thanks man," Trey smiled then stood up and watched Kaleel do the same.

"Are you good now?" Kaleel asked.

Trey nodded then hugged Kaleel.

"Yeah, I'm good now, Godfather," Trey said proudly then watched the world's biggest smile grow across Kaleel's face.

"Aha." Kaleel laughed feeling honoured inside. He stepped back then reminded Trey, "I'm still waiting to be best man at your wedding."

"Aha, you will be don't worry," Trey reassured him as he made his way to the front door. "I'll leave you to finish up. Just make sure that she isn't late to work." Trey teased as he opened the door before he made his way to the car.

***

Trey closed the front door behind him and made his way into the living room to see the lamp is on, as well as the TV which is flickering on Ayisha's body as she sleeps on the sofa. He smiled

116

to himself as he watched his queen and now the mother of his child sleeping peacefully. He walked over to the sofa, picked up the remote from the glass table in front of the sofa, and turned off the TV. He placed the remote back down, then sat beside Ayisha and kissed her cheek. Feeling her cheek being kissed and sensing her king's presence, she slowly opened her eyes then stretched as she asked,

"Was I snoring?"

He laughed after her question then watched her sit up.

"Yeah, you were shaking the whole house." Trey teased.

"I've just been sooo tired lately," Ayisha complained. She listened to Trey laugh, then looked at the TV blankly, "I'm sure I had that on."

Trey laughed again then told her,

"You did, I've just turned it off." He then moved closer to her and reached for her feet as he said, "Lay down let me give you a massage." He watched her smile then sit comfortably resting her legs on his lap.

"Thank you, baby," Ayisha said gratefully while wiggling her toes.

"Anything for my queen," Trey answered then started to massage her feet. After a few minutes of massaging each foot, Trey said to Ayisha,

"I told Kaleel you're pregnant."

Ayisha opened her eyes and asked in a relaxed and calm tone,

"What did he say?" Remembering Kaleel's reaction resulted in an even bigger smile growing across his face.

"He was excited. I told him he's going to be his or her Godfather." Trey told her proudly.

Ayisha sniggered then replied,

"I should have guessed... but it would have been nice if you asked me first."

Wondering if he had upset her, Trey asked quickly,

"Are you mad at me?"

She sighed then answered,

"No, I'm not. He's your brother so of course he's going to be the godfather, but I would have liked us to have discussed it first."

Trey nodded agreeing with her,

"You're right. I should have asked you first."

Defensibly, Ayisha replied,

"No, you didn't have to *ask* me, Trey! It would have been nice if we could have discussed it before that's all. We're both having this baby, which means we're a team. We should be able to discuss things together as a couple, as his or her parents." Trey nodded then watched Ayisha rub her stomach which melted his heart. He continued to massage her feet then said dreadfully,

"Okay, you're right. If we do have a girl, then I will have no say in this house."

Ayisha chuckled and agreed,

"That's right, if we do end up having a girl then she's going to have you wrapped around her little finger."

Trey laughed dreadfully,

"I know, but if we end up having a boy then I'm bringing him to the gym with me. I'll have him lifting weights before his first birthday." Ayisha laughed loudly until he asked, "so what are you thinking? Do you want to do a gender reveal party?"

"No, I want to know what we're having," Ayisha answered then witnessed Trey's smile fade. Not wanting him to be upset and understanding that she will have to compromise with him eventually, she smiled then suggested, "we can always have a baby shower... we'll invite our family and friends, nothing too big. We could hire a hall and do some fun baby themed games." Liking everything that Ayisha had just said, Trey smiled again as he started to picture the event. "How does that sound?"

"Sounds great, we could hire a bouncing castle, a few clowns, we could even hire a few zoo animals like Lions and Tigers," Trey suggested getting carried away with his ideas.

"Maybe... we'll figure that out once we get closer to the time. When should we start telling everyone?"

"We could call your parents then we'll call Claire after."

"Or... why don't we just invite them over and tell them together?"

"That's an even better idea! I'll call Claire first then we'll invite your parents after." Ayisha agreed then watched Trey pull his phone out. They both listen to the loud ringing sound coming from Trey's phone, as they waited for Claire to answer.

It rang two more times before Claire answered,

"Hi son, how are you?"

"I'm really good thanks. I'm just here with Ayisha how are you?" Trey said whilst looking down at his phone that he's holding in the air between them so Ayisha could hear.

"That's fantastic I'm really glad that she's back, how is my daughter in law?"

"Hey, I'm okay but Trey has something he needs to ask you," Ayisha answered.

"What is it son? Do you need me to remove that demon from your house? Is she still there? I hope not Trey!"

"Nope, she's not here anymore," Trey informed her.

"Thank you Jesus! So, what is it you've got to ask me?" Claire asked.

"We're wondering if you can come to the house tomorrow," Trey said.

"Of course, but what time? Because I don't finish work until 5 pm."

Trey looked at Ayisha as she asked,

"7pm?"

"Yeah, that's fine, I'll make my way to yours straight from work, but I'll be hungry so make sure you have something hot for me to eat," Claire requested.

"No problem, we've got you," Ayisha answered then winked at Trey. "How does curry goat with white rice and some homemade coleslaw sound?"

At the same time, Claire and Trey said,

"That's great."

Ayisha laughed then replied,

"Okay, we'll have your plate ready as soon as you get here. See you tomorrow,"

"See that's why I like you and okay thank you, I'll see you both tomorrow." Claire said then ended the call. Ayisha looked over at the glass table, looking for her phone.

"I can't remember where I put my phone," Ayisha confessed as she began to panic.

"Calm down, you probably put it on charge," Trey guessed. Ayisha nodded with a slight sigh, then rested her back against the sofa. "You can always call your parents on my phone," Trey offered. Ayisha nodded then watched him call Leroy, before handing her the phone. She pressed the loudspeaker option then waited for him to answer.

"Hi Trey," Leroy answered in a not so keen tone.

"It's me dad," Ayisha said with a smile on her face feeling warm inside from hearing his voice.

"Baby girl," Leroy called cheerfully, "how are you? When did you get back?" Leroy quizzed feeling a massive sense of relief, knowing she is safe and back where she belongs.

"Ayisha? How is she?" Tanya shouted excitedly in the background before demanding that Leroy put the call on loudspeaker. "Ayisha?" Tanya called.

"Hi mom and dad, I got back yesterday. You'll be glad to hear that Trey and I have worked everything out."

"Aww baby, I'm so glad you're back we missed you so much," Tanya told her joyfully.

"I missed you both too. I just had to get away and sort my head out which I did do, well sort of. You both will be happy to know that Chyna has finally gone for good!"

"Fantastic! When can we see you?" Leroy asked.

"Actually, that's why we're calling, we want to invite you both over here tomorrow."

"What time?" Leroy asked needing an answer.

"For 7pm?" Ayisha asked.

"I've got a meeting tomorrow with some of my business partners, I fly out at half 3 in the afternoon," Leroy informed them.

"But dad this is really important to me I need you both here." Ayisha pleaded.

Hearing the seriousness in Ayisha's voice made Tanya tell Leroy,

"She clearly needs us so you're going to cancel or rearrange that meeting."

"But it's very important I can't miss it," Leroy argued.

Not allowing Leroy to finish his sentence, Tanya interrupted him and stated,

"Listen, baby girl, your father and I will be there tomorrow for 7pm," before she reached forward and ended their call.

***

Ayisha laid out the table in the dining room, making sure everything is presented well and ready for when their parents arrive.

"What else do you need me to do?" Trey offered as he stood by the door watching Ayisha straighten the cutlery.

"Get the juice out of the fridge and bring in a bottle of wine," Ayisha ordered calmly as she stepped back and examined the table, checking to see if anything was out of place.

"Okay," Trey nodded then disappeared, trying his best to do as he was told and not get in the way. The sound of the doorbell ringing travelled through the house and hit Trey and Ayisha's eardrums.

"Can you get that please?" Ayisha requested. Trey made his way to the door then opened it to see Claire standing there.

"Hi Ma, how was work?" Trey asked.

"Hi son," Claire greeted Trey with a hug and kiss then closed the door behind her. "It was really good, we rehomed one of the boys today which was lovely to see, he's been wanting a family for a few years now and today he finally got one."

"That's good," Trey said then watched Claire walk over to the bottom of the stairs. "Where are you going?" He asked curiously.

"To check that Chyna has really gone," Claire said sceptically.

Trey laughed then reassured her,

"You won't find her up there so there's no need to check."

"Boy hush up, I just need to see for myself," Claire said then disappeared upstairs. Shaking his head, Trey laughed as he stood at the bottom of the stairs waiting for Claire to return. After a few more seconds of waiting, Claire suddenly appeared at the top of the stairs and began to make her way back down, with a big smile on her face.

"Did you find her hiding in the bathroom?" Trey teased.

"No, and you're lucky I didn't!" Claire answered then nudged Trey once she reached the bottom of the stairs. "What's that smell?" Claire asked as she sniffed the combinations of smells, from herbs to the Caribbean seasonings.

"That would be your special request," Trey hinted as they walked into the kitchen.

"I smell curry goat," Claire stated as she made her way over to Ayisha, who is standing in front of the stove stirring the food.

"That's right I couldn't let you down," Ayisha said then closed the lid and hugged her.

"It smells lovely I can't wait to eat it," Claire said as she let go of Ayisha. "I had to have a look for myself just to make sure that Chyna is really gone."

Ayisha smiled then confessed whilst placing the wooden spoon onto the counter,

"That's all I've been doing since I've been back. Each time I used the toilet last night I kept checking the spare room, just to make sure she wasn't there."

"Aww bless ya, that's how much of a disease that poor girl was. I'm just glad she's finally out of your lives and hopefully for good," Claire said.

"Amen to that," Ayisha agreed then heard the doorbell go off.

"That's got to be Tanya and Leroy," Trey guessed then looked at Ayisha's nervous face. She is excited to see her parents, but she's unsure if they will both be turning up.

"Hi son." Tanya greeted Trey with a warm hug.

"Hi, thanks for coming," Trey said then stepped out of Tanya's hug before shaking Leroy's hand.

"Hi Trey, where is Ayisha?" Leroy asked as he stepped inside the house and stood in the middle of the entrance.

"Ayisha's in the kitchen," Trey said as he turned around and saw Ayisha running towards them.

"You came!" Ayisha said cheerfully as she jumped into Leroy's arms. Tanya stood there smiling as she watched her husband and daughter hug for ages.

"Is Claire here?" Tanya asked as she looked away from them to look at Trey.

Creeping towards them, Claire said,

"Yes, I am."

"Hey!" Tanya greeted Claire with a hug and kiss.

***

Leroy sat at the head of the table while Ayisha sat next to Tanya, and Trey sat next to Claire. They are all enjoying their food so much that only the sound of their silver cutlery hitting off the ceramic plates can be heard.

Finishing what is in her mouth, Claire said,

"Thank God that no mannered child is out of this house."

Agreeing with Claire, Tanya said,

"Amen, I still can't believe they agreed to take her in."

Feeling agitated, Ayisha said,

"It seemed like a good idea at the time, but she's gone now so can we stop talking about her."

"Amen to that." Claire agreed then raised her glass and looked at everyone to do the same. They all picked up their glasses as Claire toasted, "to Chyna leaving."

Leroy nodded then took a sip of his drink before he heard Tanya say,

"Now that she's gone you can work on giving me some grandbabies." Ayisha looked at Trey then smiled asking if she could tell them. He smiled back then nodded, giving her the go ahead.

"We could, but there's no point because I'm already pregnant," Ayisha announced with a chuffed expression.

"What?" Tanya and Claire said at the same time.

"Yep, she's pregnant," Trey confirmed as he looked at Claire with a proud look on his face.

"Wow," Claire said then pulled Trey into her hug and squeezed him.

"Congratulations baby," Tanya said as she felt her eyes fill with tears of joy. As happy as she is, Tanya couldn't bring herself to move. She knew how much Ayisha had dreamed of this all happening and now that it is, she couldn't help but freeze.

"You're going to be a grandma," Ayisha said then reached for Tanya's hand and held it, understanding she is overwhelmed.

"Congratulations," Leroy said to Ayisha. He looked directly at Trey before he hinted, "don't you think it's about time that you made your relationship more official with Ayisha?"

"Yes sir," Trey nodded.

"How far are you?" Claire asked curiously.

"11 weeks," Ayisha answered.

"11 weeks," Tanya echoed as she looked at Leroy who smiled at her. "They're having a baby." She told him.

"They are." Leroy agreed then winked at her.

"Wow, I can't believe my baby's having a baby." Claire said while rubbing Trey's back. "I know it's still early but what do you think you're having?" They all thought for a few seconds then started guessing whether it will be a boy or girl.

"You're definitely carrying just one, aren't you?" Tanya asked.

"Yes, just one." Ayisha giggled then looked at Trey who is lost in his thoughts - imagining how their life would be with twins.

"Trey," Leroy called, disturbing him from daydreaming,

"What do you think you're having?"

Trey stuttered as he adjusted to being back in the room then guessed,

"A boy?"

"Aww, that would be lovely," Claire said as she pictured Trey's younger face.

"How far have you got with the planning? Have you started to decorate the room yet? Have you thought of any names?" Tanya asked getting excited.

"Oh yes, what about baby names? I've always liked Lorenzo or Lauren?" Claire suggested.

"I like Reece or Courtney," Tanya suggested also.

"We haven't thought of any names yet," Ayisha said quickly. Trey looks at Ayisha and can see how overwhelmed she is becoming. Not wanting their parents to get too ahead of themselves, Trey summarised,

"We haven't started any decorating or shopping yet, it's all still new to us but we're going to start soon."

"Don't worry about that, we're going to help you out," Tanya said then pulled out her phone. "I know an interior designer. I'll give her a call and she'll happily decorate the room for you."

Watching Tanya unlock her phone, Trey cleared his throat and insisted nervously,

"It's okay, we'll sort it out."

"Don't be silly this is our first grandchild, we've got this!" Tanya insisted.

"Honestly, it's okay Ma," Ayisha insisted then watched Tanya look for the designer's number.

Missing their hint, Tanya continued to insist,

"It's fine baby, once I've contacted the designer, I'll find you an event planner for a gender reveal."

"No, it's okay," Ayisha said then heard Claire say,

"While you do that, I'll find my friend's number because she specialises in home births."

"NO, WE'RE FINE!" Ayisha yelled as she banged her hands on the table. Leroy, Tanya and Claire gasped as they looked at Ayisha in shock. They watched her jump up from her seat then stomp out the living room before running up the stairs heavily.

Once Ayisha left the room, all their shocked and questioning eyes made their way back over to Trey.

"Sorry... um, it's just that we haven't discussed everything yet." Trey said before he wiped his mouth with his napkin. "I think it's best for us to call it a night," Trey suggested then watched them all stand up slowly.

"Should I check on her?" Tanya offered unsurely.

"Maybe not today, I think we should leave her to Trey," Leroy paused then looked directly at him, "you've got this haven't you?"

Hearing the seriousness in his voice, Trey nodded then told him,

"I do," before he walked them all to the door.

"I'm sorry for upsetting Ayisha, please let her know that I said goodbye," Claire said as she kissed Trey on his cheek.

"It's okay and I will," Trey said then helped Claire to put on her coat.

"Good night," Claire said before she hugged Leroy and Tanya then left.

"Please let her know I'm sorry, I will call her in the morning just to make sure she's okay." Tanya said with an upset look on her face.

"I will do, she'll be fine she just needs some time to cool down," Trey said then hugged her.

"I know she will," Tanya said then stepped out of their hug.

"Look after her," Leroy said with a serious look on his face.

"I will," Trey said then shook his hand.

Leroy smiled then said,

"Congratulations son."

Trey made his way up the stairs and headed into their room. He gently tapped on the door then tiptoed in. There lay Ayisha on their bed with a wet face and red eyes. She sat up then wiped away her tears as she watched Trey walk over to the bed. He sat down and rested his back against the headboard before he pulled her close to him. Letting him pull her, she rested her head on his lap.

"Are you okay?" Trey finally asked breaking the silence.

Ayisha sniffled then rubbed her stomach as she sighed, "I think so."

"Think? What's the matter? They were just trying to help." Trey defended their parents' actions.

"I know they were I feel so silly now," Ayisha answered. Deciding to listen to his heart, Trey asked,

"Are you sure that's the reason why you got so upset?"

Ayisha turned her head to look up at him, then asked,

"What made you ask that?"

"Because... they were just offering to help, not once did they say anything that could have gotten you that upset."

"They were taking over!" Ayisha moaned as she sat up to face him.

"I know they were, but I saw your face when Leroy spoke about marriage, you suddenly changed, so what is it?" Ayisha stared at him with a blank look on her face. She is impressed that Trey knows her so well but refused to answer the question.

"Are you scared of having this baby?" Trey guessed.

"No, well yeah, but that's not it," Ayisha said.

"Then what is it?" Ayisha looked away from Trey then looked around their room. She looked at their pictures that hang on the walls, then looked back at him before she said,

"It's just... this isn't how I pictured it."

"Pictured what?" Trey asked then looked at their pictures, unsure of how to take what he had just heard.

"This wasn't how I pictured us, this, my life, our life together."

"What do you mean?" Trey asked desperate to understand what she meant.

"I mean... I imagined us living happily married together before we even started a family. But instead, I'm living and sleeping in a room you once shared with someone else. Someone you had already planned on being with for the rest of your life." Ayisha confessed finally feeling a sense of relief from speaking her mind. Not knowing how exactly to take what he had just heard, Trey said,

"That's the past. Chyna's gone and she's not coming back. She's out of our lives for good. I'm not quite sure what to suggest... we could always sell the house... then find somewhere else to live." Trey suggested wholeheartedly.

"No, I don't want you to do that," Ayisha said.

"Then what? I'm not sure what to do here. I'm trying to compromise with you but I'm not quite sure what you're trying to say."

Ayisha sighed then said,

"Neither do I... it's just that this isn't how I pictured my life when I was younger. This isn't how we planned our lives together."

"Ayisha, we're not kids any more shit happens. You moved away, and I thought I'd never see you again, so I did what I had to do. We really need to stop thinking about the past and focus on the now and our future together," Trey said then pointed at her stomach, "you're carrying our future in there so the last thing you need to be doing is stressing. Chyna has gone and she's never coming back so you need to accept it." Ayisha nodded then agreed with him. "Come here," Trey said as he pulled her close to him and hugged her. "Chyna's gone now. I think it's about time we focus on us and our family."

***

Trey and Ayisha are cuddling, enjoying each other's company. They reminisced on how they planned their lives together when they were kids, then discussed how they plan on raising their first child and the principles they're going to teach him or her. As he lay there listening to Ayisha, something randomly overcame him.

Interrupting her from talking, Trey asks,

"Marry me?"

"What?" Ayisha asked then sat up to look at him, to see if he was serious or not, "did you just ask me to marry you?"

"I did," Trey smiled then explained himself, "I don't want to be anywhere else but here right now with you. I loved you from when we were kids and now that I've got you, I want to keep you forever, I don't care how selfish that sounds."

Ayisha giggled then said,

"Well, this isn't how I pictured your proposal either."

Agreeing with her, Trey said,

"I know but it just feels right, so will you marry me?"

Ayisha smiled then grabbed hold of his face with both hands and kissed him.

"Of course I will," Ayisha shouted.

With the world's biggest smile on his face, Trey told her,

"I'll buy you an engagement ring tomorrow, Mrs Waterhouse."

"Oh, don't worry about that there's no rush, but Mrs Waterhouse, I like the sound of that!"

***

Trey held the door open for Ayisha then watched her walk into the consulting room and greet the doctor.

"Look at you missy, you're glowing." Doctor Parkinson said as she stepped out of their hug and admired her glowing skin. Doctor Parkinson is a close friend of Ayisha's parents. After sitting their parents down and talking to them about being too hands-on, Tanya, Leroy and Claire agreed to back off and to only give their advice when needed. With the condition that Trey and

Ayisha agreed to have Doctor Parkinson look after them, so Tanya could be assured her grandchild is in the best hands.

"Thank you," Ayisha said as she walked over to the chair. After hugging Trey, Doctor Parkinson made her way over to her desk and sat down. She opened Ayisha's details on her desktop then asked them energetically,

"Are you excited to find out the sex of your baby?"

"Yeah, I can't wait," Trey said as he helped Ayisha take off her coat.

"Fantastic," Doctor Parkinson said as she watched them. She then got up and instructed them to, "join me over here once you're ready," as she washed her hands. Ayisha walked over to the hydraulic chair then climbed onto it. Once Ayisha was resting comfortably, she rolled up her top and heard the doctor ask Trey, "what are you hoping for a boy or a girl?"

"As long as it's healthy then I'm fine, but I'm hoping for a boy," Trey answered then heard Ayisha say,

"He only wants a boy so he can have another gym partner."

"Well, let's have a look." Doctor Parkinson said then retrieved the ultrasound gel and squeezed some onto the lower part of Ayisha's stomach. She laughed as the cold clear and thick gel sent a cold tingling sensation across her stomach.

"It's cold," Ayisha stated then tensed as the doctor used the ultrasound probe to spread the gel around her stomach.

"Everyone says that," The Doctor said as she laughed. Trey and Ayisha gazed at the screen, watching and waiting to find out the gender of their baby. As Ayisha felt the probe being moved around on her stomach, they heard the doctor announce proudly, "it looks like you're both having a healthy baby... girl." Ayisha clapped joyfully as Trey sucked his teeth then started to laugh.

"I definitely won't have a say in the house," Trey stated then watched the doctor and Ayisha laugh together.

"Who runs the world? Girls!" Ayisha sang as she looked at Trey, teasing him.

"Yeah, yeah," Trey laughed then held Ayisha's hand.

"Well, congratulations on your healthy baby girl," Doctor Parkinson said, "have you thought of any names yet?"

"I was hoping for a boy, so we thought of Treyvon," Trey answered.

"But we're having a girl so we're going with Aria," Ayisha said proudly.

"That's a beautiful name Tanya will love that." Doctor Parkinson stated as she cleaned Ayisha's stomach.

"Thank you," Ayisha grinned.

***

Trey parked outside of Tanya and Leroy's mansion but left the engine running. Excitedly, Ayisha got out straight away then noticed Trey hadn't moved.

"Aren't you coming in?" Ayisha asked.

"Nah, I'm going to chill with Kaleel," Trey answered.

"Are you sure?"

"Yeah, I'm sure. I'm going to call Claire then go to the gym after."

"Okay, love you," Ayisha said then rushed to the door ready to tell her parents the good news. Still parked outside, Trey unlocked his phone and called Claire. He waited a few seconds before she answered,

"Hey son, I'm at work so I can't talk for long."

"Oh okay, I just rang to let you know that we found out what we're having."

"Really? What is it a boy or a girl?" Claire asked. Trey waited for a few seconds then announced,

"We're having a girl." Claire screamed down the phone joyfully, making him laugh. "Have a guess what we're going to name her."

"Oh, I don't know, tell me son, I need to know!" Claire pleaded unable to control her excitement anymore.

"Aria-Leigh Waterhouse."

"Wow son, I love it that's really a beautiful name. I'm going to tell everyone at work." Claire said then hung up before he could thank her or even say goodbye. He laughed to himself as he shook his head then made his way to the gym.

***

Trey walked through the automatic doors then made his way over to the desk, where Cardi is on her mobile phone. Sensing a presence approaching, she locked it then looked up to see Trey giving her an evil look.

"Welcome home Trey," She said.

"Yeah, yeah, don't give me that. You cheated on me with my homeboy," Trey said with a smirk on his face.

She chuckled then said,

"I mean, you've got Ayisha now I had to think tactically."

"So, if I was a free man then we'd be together?"

"Of course, just look at you!" She answered then watched him flex his muscles.

"Now watch me walk off into the sunset," Trey teased as he did the famous 'Terry Crew's walk'.

"Brother!" Trey called Kaleel who is training Terry.

"Hey!" Kaleel responded then watched him walk over.

"I was just talking to your girl," Trey told Kaleel as they hugged.

"What was she saying?" Kaleel asked as he watched Trey and Terry hug.

"Nothing much, just that if I wasn't with Ayisha then her and I would be together."

"Is that right?" Kaleel laughed then leaned against the wall.

"Mm, but all jokes aside, I walked in on her using her phone. Just cause she's dating the manager doesn't mean she can start doing as she pleases; I don't want her to start slacking." Trey said in a concerned tone.

"Don't worry about it I'll talk to her," Kaleel said then spotted Trey's natural glow, "what's this glow all about?"

With a massive smile growing across his face he told them both,

"We found out we're having a girl."

"Congrats!" Kaleel and Terry said at the same time.

"So much for us having another gym partner," Terry said then asked, "how are you feeling?"

"I'm good, the baby's healthy so that's all that matters. But it's got me thinking about all the boys I'm going to fight off. She's not allowed to have a boyfriend until she's 30." Trey stated.

"Definitely, matter of fact make that 40!" Kaleel corrected him.

"That poor girl," Terry laughed then asked, "have you thought of any names yet?"

"Yeah, Aria-Leigh Waterhouse." Trey told them proudly.

"Nice," Terry nodded.

"I like it but where did the Leigh come from? Y'all got some Chinese in the family I haven't met yet?" Kaleel asked.

Trey shrugged then confessed,

"Nah, it just sounds nice."

They all laughed together until Trey told them, "she's 20 weeks it's gone so fast."

"It will do but it sounds like you've both got everything under control," Terry said then asked, "what did Claire say?"

"She likes the name, she screamed down the phone then hung up to tell everyone at work," Trey laughed.

"Yeah, she's always loved kids it's a shame she couldn't have any herself." Terry said then felt the mood change.

134

**

After working up a sweat, they all gasped for their breaths then gulped down some water.

While still gasping Trey said to Terry,

"Even though you've been back in my life for a few months now, I feel like we've really bonded," Trey paused then watched Terry smile. "We're planning on having a baby shower and I would like it if you could come."

Terry's eyes widened in shock then asked curiously, "When?"

"We haven't set a date yet but once we have, I'll let you know, will you be able to come?"

Kaleel looked at Trey then said,

"I know it's not really my place to say... I can see that you've bonded and all which is good, but you're forgetting about Claire. Do you really think having him there will be a good idea?"

"He's back in my life now and I want him to be in my daughter's life too. He's a wise man and I actually think he's a good person." Trey said which made Terry smile.

"I appreciate the invitation and I completely understand Kaleel's concern; I'll think about it," Terry said as he thought about Claire.

"It's nothing against you but I just thought I'd mention it." Kaleel justified himself to Terry.

"I didn't think of that, but they're both adults so they should be able to act accordingly," Trey said.

"I can, but I can't guarantee how Claire will act when she sees me... so I'll think about it but thanks for the offer," Terry said gratefully.

Aria's baby shower:

Ayisha's standing in front of the mirror looking at her reflection. She is wearing a long white strapless dress with white sliders to match. She refused to wear her high heels and planned to be as comfortable as possible. Even though she hardly ever wore makeup, she decided to apply a bit of lipstick just to uplift her mood.

"I look like a whale wearing a shower curtain," Ayisha complained to Trey as he entered their room.

"Don't be silly you look beautiful!" Trey said then rushed over to her and rubbed her stomach. "Remember you're carrying my princess in there."

"I can't forget that," Ayisha moaned then told him, "I don't want everyone touching my stomach today."

"Okay, if I see anyone trying to, then I'll stop them," Trey said protectively. Sensing Ayisha is having an off day, and not wanting her to stay that way Trey said, "hey, listen, you look beautiful I wish you can see what I see. Today is our day and everyone has travelled and taken time out of their day just to see us and celebrate Princess Aria."

"I know, I just feel fat," Ayisha complained.

"No, you're not! You're forgetting how hard we work out in the gym to keep you in shape, you look beautiful and even if you did look like a whale in a shower curtain, I'd still love you."

Ayisha chuckled slightly then hugged him. "Come on let's do this for Aria," Trey said then walked towards the door.

"Aria-Leigh Waterhouse." Ayisha corrected him with a growing smile on her face.

***

Trey held the door open for Ayisha then followed behind her into the hall. The room is filled with friends and family who are chatting amongst themselves. They walked through the crowd while being congratulated and hugged.

"Congratulations Trey," Jamie said - one of the kids from the hub.

"Thanks little man. You know I'm having a girl right? So, I'm going to need a lot of help fighting off all the boys." Trey said then listened to them all chant, confirming his question.

"Are you ready to be a dad?" Kendrick asked before the chanting faded. Trey looked around at their tuned in faces who listened carefully for an answer. They idolise him and look up to him as their elder brother. They love how hands-on and involved he is in their lives and take his words seriously.

"I guess I'm as ready as I'll ever be, but I've got you guys to help me out. Who's helping me change her nappies?" They all screwed up their faces and laughed after him, refusing to help him out. "Alright, thanks for coming I'm just going to say hello to everyone else. There's plenty of food and drinks so help yourselves and eat as much as you want." Trey said as he walked off into the crowd.

"Ayisha," Tanya called. She is standing with Leroy and Ayisha's side of the family.

"Hey," Ayisha waved then walked over to them.

"Look at you," Tanya said as she hugged her then rubbed her stomach, "how are you?"

"I'm okay now, I was hormonal this morning but seeing everyone here has cheered me up," Ayisha answered then looked past Tanya, at her grandmother who is sitting in her wheelchair. "Grandma," Ayisha called as she walked over to her, bent down then gave her a hug. "It's really nice to see you, I wasn't expecting to see you here," Ayisha confessed.

"I maybe 91 but there's no way I was going to miss my Great-Granddaughters baby shower." She said in her tired and weak voice. "Where is your fiancé?"

"Aww, thank you and Trey's around somewhere, we've just got here so he's probably speaking to his family, but I will introduce you to him later."

"Great, I can't wait."

Trey finished talking to his cousins then decided to have a look around the hall. He and Ayisha had agreed to let their parents organise the baby shower. He walked over to the table that has pink cupcakes and snacks neatly placed on both sides of the cake. The cake is a custom pink cot with a brown skinned doll in the centre of it. He laughed to himself, then looked at the other tables that have presents stacked up to the ceiling. There is so many that some are shoved under the table and stacked on the floor. He attempted to walk over to the table and take a cupcake until he felt his shoulder being tapped.

"Congrats brother," Kaleel said over the music that is being played in the background. Trey turned around then hugged him while thanking him for coming. "No problem, I wasn't going to miss my Goddaughters baby shower," Kaleel stated then looked over to the table.

"Have you seen the cake?" Kaleel stepped closer to the table and inspected it with his eyes.

"Is that really a doll in there?" Kaleel asked in disbelief.

"It is," Trey confirmed, "they went all out didn't they?"

"They really did!" Kaleel agreed before they both looked around at the decorations. "Is that really a baby-shaped balloon?"

"Yeah, it is," Trey laughed then heard Kaleel confess,

"I thought they only made round balloons."

"So did I," Trey agreed as he leant forward and handed Kaleel a pink cupcake.

"Thanks, I'm sure this is a good excuse for a cheat day." Kaleel said then heard Claire say,

"Eh, I hope I get one too."

"Hey Ma," Trey said then turned around to hug her.

"Where's Ayisha?" Claire asked as she stepped out of their hug.

Trey shrugged then answered,

"We lost each other; she's probably speaking to her family." As Claire's eyes scanned the room looking for Ayisha, her eyes spotted a familiar face that she hasn't seen in years.

"Is that Terry?" Claire asked with a shocked look on her face like she has just seen a ghost. Trey looked in the same direction to where Claire is looking, then spotted Terry walking over to them. He took a few steps closer to Terry then hugged and thanked him for coming, with Claire watching in shock.

"What is he doing here?" Claire interrogated Trey, ignoring Terry.

"Hi Claire," Terry said as he looked directly at her. Acting like he is invisible, Claire ignored him then looked at Trey evilly which confirmed to Kaleel this was a bad idea.

"Outside now!" Claire demanded then marched towards the exit, seeing through anyone that was in her way.

Ayisha stood in the middle of the hall with her friend's listening to their horror stories of childbirth, when a group of people making their way towards the exit caught her attention. Desperate for a reason to leave, Ayisha looked harder to see its Trey. Politely removing herself from the conversation, Ayisha headed towards the door and followed Claire, Trey, Kaleel and Terry out of the hall.

"What is he doing here?" Claire questioned Trey getting straight to the point. Trey stood there helplessly with a guilty look on his face, unable to speak or defend himself. He bowed his head, refusing to make any eye contact with Claire. Ayisha joined them outside to see Claire had an angry expression on her face and Trey had completely shut down. Unaware of what is happening, Ayisha walked over to them and stood next to Kaleel. She looked at Kaleel who is standing there watching helplessly.

"What's happening?" Ayisha whispered. As Kaleel informed her, Terry said to Claire,

"Don't be mad at Trey it's not his fault it's mine. I was the one that asked to come today." Stopping herself from confronting Terry, Claire took a few deep breaths desperately trying to calm herself down, before she yelled not too loudly,

"Don't tell me what to do or how to act!"

"Okay," Terry replied as he watched her stand there calculating something in her head. Realising what Terry had just said, Claire looked over to Trey then shouted,

"How does he know about the baby shower? Wait, have you guys... WHEN DID YOU BOTH BECOME BEST FRIENDS?" She is angry because she knew Trey and Terry had crossed paths at his gym, but she was unaware of how close they have become, which made her feel betrayed by them both. She is also upset because this is the first time, she has seen Terry in over 19 years. Seeing him brought back all those mixed emotions on how she felt the day she got home to see that all his belongings had gone, to receiving their divorce papers, to the hate she developed towards him from their nasty break up.

"Not here, let's talk somewhere else," Terry suggested as he stepped closer to Claire, grabbed hold of her arm and attempted to gently pull her away from the entrance of the hall.

"DON'T TOUCH ME!" Claire exclaimed then yanked her arm away from his hand. As she felt his flesh touching her precious body that he no longer owned, angered her even more. Without thinking, she stepped back then swung her arm and slapped his chubby cheek. They all gasped as they heard Claire's palm and Terry's cheek connect.

"Ma!" Trey called then pulled Claire away from him.

Seeing how quickly the situation had escalated, Ayisha stepped back then shielded her stomach while Kaleel stepped forward and pulled Terry away.

"Don't touch me!" Claire shouted then pushed Trey away from her.

"Ma," Trey called in a disheartened tone.

"You betrayed me son," Claire said with an aching heart.

"I can't believe you invited this clown knowing damn well how much I despise him." Not wanting the situation to escalate any further and for Aria's baby shower to turn into an episode of Jerry Springer, Kaleel decided to interrupt and tell Claire,

"Terry turned up at the gym randomly, he had no idea Trey owned it. He apologised which Trey decided to accept and over time they got to know each other."

Claire looked away from Kaleel then said to Trey,

"I can't believe you've done this to me. When were you going to tell me?"

Trey shrugged then confessed,

"I don't know," before he bowed his head again. Ayisha can see how upset her fiancé is and how hurt her mother in law is, so she rushed over to Trey and comforted him while saying to them,

"This isn't the time or the place for this! This is your first grandchild's baby shower let's not ruins this celebration." They all nodded agreeing with Ayisha apart from Claire.

"I'm sorry but I can't be under the same roof as that excuse of a man, so I'll just leave," Claire said without looking at Terry.

"No Ma, please don't go," Trey pleaded. Terry looked at Trey to see the hurt and pain in his eyes. As grateful as he was for Trey inviting him, he knew it was best for him to go. He accepted the part he had played in their lives and understands why Claire is so hostile towards him.

He opened his mouth then quietly said,

"No, don't leave, I'll go," before he looked at Ayisha and Trey then apologised, "I'm sorry for ruining your day and I hope it gets better."

"Okay, thank you and thanks for coming," Ayisha spoke for Trey, then they watched Terry turn away and walk off.

"I'm sorry Ma," Trey apologised then stepped closer to Claire and attempted to hug her.

"It's okay," Claire sighed as she hugged him back, "you lot go back inside, and I'll join you all once I've calmed down."

"Are you sure you're going to come back in?" Trey asked.

"Yes, go in," Claire insisted then pushed Trey towards the entrance of the hall. "I just need a breather."

"Okay, we'll see you inside," Ayisha said then grabbed Kaleel's arms and followed Trey inside.

"Sit down here," Tanya said as she held Ayisha's hand and led the way over to two chairs that are positioned in the middle of the hall. The music began to fade as everyone gathered around, giving Trey and Ayisha their full attention.

"We're not opening all those presents today are we?" Trey asked dreadfully because there are more than 200 presents.

"No silly, just half of them," Tanya said then rushed over to the table and gathered the smallest presents. She rushed back over to them then handed them two presents each to open first. They all watched Ayisha open the first one with half of the audience holding their phones recording.

"Aww, thank you," Ayisha said gratefully as she pulled the tiniest pair of black and pink Jordan's she has ever seen out of the wrapping paper.

"They're so small," Trey stated as his eyes registered the size and compared it to Ayisha's hands.

"I know right, what's in that?" Ayisha asked as she looked at the wrapped spongey present that Trey's holding in his hand.

"Let's see," Trey said as he started to tear the wrapping paper then dropped the shredded pieces onto the floor. Once it's fully unwrapped, he unfolds the tiny baseball jacket with red stitching on the back that says, 'Da hubs no.1 girl.' A massive smile grew across Trey's face as he guessed who it's from. He looked into the crowd of tuned in and proud eyes, then heard the kids from the hub chant proudly.

"Aww, that's lovely thank you," Ayisha said then blinked in sync with a few camera flashes.

"Thanks," Trey said to them all then handed the jacket to Tanya to hold. He picked up the rectangular box from his lap then pulled off the blue ribbon. He smirked, knowing the kids from the hub had pulled a prank on him. He raised the lid then muttered, "what the heck?" as his eyes registered what is inside the jewellery box. "Is this a joke or something?" Trey asked Ayisha who is just as shocked as he is.

"No, that's not mine," Ayisha insisted before they all heard someone from the crowd say,

"It's mine." One by one everyone looked behind them. Unsure of what is going on, Trey and Ayisha look through the crowd, then watch everyone suddenly move and form a walking path.

"You've got to be kidding me!" Claire barked as her eyes followed the body walk through the gap that was created. As the crowd gasped, Trey stuttered as he spotted a light-skinned female with blue curly hair appear.

"What's she doing here?" A voice from the crowd asked before Kendrick shouted,

"She's gone fat!"

"Hi Trey!" Chyna said as her eyes connected with his. She watched him slowly stand up whilst holding the box with a positive pregnancy test in his hand. He tried his best to speak but his body and mind prevented him. The shock of seeing Chyna turn up at their baby shower, with an even bigger bump than Ayisha's is too much for her. She sat there physically frozen with her eyes wide open as she looks at Chyna's swollen cheeks and round belly. As the realisation hit her, Ayisha felt her mouth fill with saliva, so she covered her mouth with one hand, then stood up with everything on her lap falling onto the floor. Trying her best not to be sick in front of everyone, Ayisha kicked the wrapping paper out of her way, then ran to the bathroom with Tanya and her closest friend's following behind. Trey watched Ayisha run off but was unable to move or chase after her. His feet felt like they're glued to the floor.

"Congratulations," Chyna said as she stood there rubbing her stomach and looking around the room at the pink decorations. As much as Trey wanted to say something back, he couldn't. Only the music in the background could be heard along with the shocked random muttering from the crowd. Chyna looked around the room at all the gob-smacked faces and the phones that are still recording. She smirked to herself, then looked back at Trey who is still standing there with wide eyes and an open mouth. Understanding he isn't able to speak, Chyna decided to ask him, "do you like the blue ribbon on your present? If you haven't guessed already, we're having a boy."

TO BE CONTINUED...

Thank you for reading I hope you really enjoyed this story.
Please feel free to leave an honest review. I also welcome positive criticism.

Part 3 is now out! Search for 'Success with my wife to be'

You can find me on social media:
Instagram: www.instagram.com/Cassiscreative
Personal Instagram: www.instagram.com/Kissandrah
Facebook: www.facebook.com/Cassiscreative
Facebook Group: Keeping Up With Cass The Author

Please be sure to tag us in any selfies or photos to do with this book or send them to us and we will feature you on our pages.
#successwiththerightqueen #SWTRQ #loveandsuccessseries #cassandradyersbooks

Printed in Great Britain
by Amazon